JAILBIRD

Many thought that John Taber would never again show his face in Charon after his prison term had been served — but appear he did. Despite determined opposition, Taber was intent on gathering enough evidence to prove he had been guiltless of the crime for which he had been sent to prison. But the desperation to drive him out of Charon before he found out things best left hidden could only end in violence and death. Would Taber survive?

Books by Tom Anson
in the Linford Western Library:

PLAGUE OF GUNFIGHTERS
THE BOUNTYMEN

TOM ANSON

JAILBIRD

Complete and Unabridged

LINFORD
Leicester

First published in Great Britain in 1998 by
Robert Hale Limited
London

First Linford Edition
published 1999
by arrangement with
Robert Hale Limited
London

The right of Tom Anson to be identified as
the author of this work has been asserted by
him in accordance with the
Copyright, Designs and Patents Act, 1988

British Library CIP Data

Anson, Tom
    Jailbird.—Large print ed.—
    Linford western library
    1. Western stories
    2. Large type books
    I. Title
    823.9′14 [F]

    ISBN 0–7089–5514–2

Published by
F. A. Thorpe (Publishing) Ltd.
Anstey, Leicestershire

Set by Words & Graphics Ltd.
Anstey, Leicestershire
Printed and bound in Great Britain by
T. J. International Ltd., Padstow, Cornwall

This book is printed on acid-free paper

1

A railroad employee wearing a hat with a peak stood alone on the platform of the Charon depot. A single lantern barely gave light to the place. Another, in the telegraph office which was housed in the depot building, contributed little more light through its grimy window.

Once again the railroad man took a worn, nickel-plated watch from a vest pocket, thumbed it open, then glanced at the big depot clock with its roman numerals, for comparison. 11.28 p.m. The Western-Trans-Territory was now a little more than twenty minutes late. Not that such a thing was unusual; it was just that tonight's train, if recent rumour turned out to be true, might be bringing in some problems for some folk hereabouts. The railroad man was not relishing the possibility of trouble when the train got in. He glanced around, eyes narrowed, as though attempting to pierce the gloom beyond the reach of the sorry lamplight. No sign of anybody. Just him and the telegraph operator in his poky office. But that did not necessarily mean anything. There had been a certain tension in the town for several days past. There had been unusually frequent comings and goings of S-Bar riders, Sam Stedman's men, and that in itself had given rise to speculation. Yet, oddly enough, during this day, the S-Bar seemed to have vanished. Their absence, however, had not diminished the general mood of apprehension.

Earlier, the telegraph operator had asked, 'Yuh reckon he'll come?' The railroad man had shrugged. How the hell would he know? At the present time all he wanted was to see in the Western-Trans-Territory and see it out again, then get on home, off this bleak depot, and the hell with all of them. The faint sound of a train whistle came through the night. The railroad man

2

walked to the end of the platform. Presently the great yellow headlamp of the train came into view, cutting the outer darkness.

If others in the town had been waiting for the wailing sound of the late train, the streets bore no evidence of it. In a couple of the saloons lamps were still glowing, and another was still lit outside the Charon County Jail.

Now the train was rolling into the depot and coming to a squeaking, clanking halt, smoke piling away into the almost windless air, steam washing out from the oil-smelling green and gold locomotive. In blue coveralls, the engineer and fireman could be seen up on the footplate. At the opposite end from the caboose, the freight conductor stepped down. The man on the depot walked across to speak to him.

For a few minutes it seemed that no one was going to get out of the one passenger car. Then the tall man was there, appearing as though out of nowhere, walking through the swirling steam, a long canvas sack shoulder-slung. He was moving in the opposite direction from the railroad men.

The freight conductor asked, 'That him?'

'Cain't be sure. From what I recall it sure does look like him.' In his heart of hearts he knew it was Taber right enough.

Behind his dirty glass, the telegraph operator caught one glimpse, poor though the lamplight was, and he too recognized the man. Hardly had Taber passed by to be swallowed up in shadow than the key was tapping out, waking a dozing operator in Shelby, sixty miles south: JOHN TABER JUST WALKED IN OFF TRANS-TERRITORY.

A tall man indeed, was Taber, but gaunt, and with a slight tendency to stoop. His hands were large. His face, stubble-whiskered, was thin, with prominent cheekbones and his slate-coloured eyes were deeply set. He was wearing narrow-legged black pants, a

4

dark-blue denim shirt with a black leather vest over it, unbuttoned, and a shallow-crowned black hat. He was wearing no pistol. When he came out on the other side of the depot, he stopped. There was no doubt in his mind that they would know he was coming. Some might have chosen not to believe it, but others would have. The fact that none of them had been at the depot when the train arrived meant nothing.

From where he now stood, he could see at the end of the short street which, at its further end, joined the main street, a faint glow from lamps still burning there. To his left and to his right, dark streets ran, these parallel to the main one and containing, as he recalled, freight yards, some corrals, storehouses of various kinds and at least one lumber yard. The street to his right would lead him to another, running at right angles, and in which, if it still existed, was a rooming-house run by a woman named Corbin. Though uncertain of the reception he would get, he had already decided to make an approach there. What he needed most right now was sleep.

Taber glanced back towards the depot. The telegraph operator withdrew slowly from his doorway. Taber, his canvas sack still slung across his shoulder, went pacing away along the street to his right. He walked as near as he could judge along the middle of that street, not hurrying, reasoning that if he had been seen by anyone other than those at the depot, he must surely hear the sounds of anyone approaching. On he walked, pausing once to glance behind him. There was only the glow coming from the region of the depot, caused not so much by the dull glow from the lanterns there as the large headlamp of the locomotive. All the same, he realized that the lightness directly behind him was strong enough to reveal his outline. Now he regretted that he had not gone the slightly longer route, using the main street.

Nonetheless he walked on. Up ahead, however, he thought that there had been a slight sound. He arrived at the intersecting street. Here, in windows, a couple of lamps were showing. Taber was standing at the corner where there was a lumber yard, the stacks limned against the lighter darkness of the sky. He turned his head slightly, listening. There had been a sound that could have been the scuffing of a boot. And another, perhaps a muttered word. Taber took a breath and prepared to move on again.

They were there right enough. Likely they had been moving ahead of him as he came along the street. They came at him out of the lumber yard and it was a moment or two before he was able to discern that there were three of them.

He would have been overwhelmed at once but for three things: he was carrying the canvas sack filled with his belongings; and, tired though he was his reflexes were sharp enough; and, the men who had come to set upon him were no more than saloon brawlers who had been drinking. That, in fact, was one of the first things he became aware of, the stink of whiskey. The men themselves stank, almost an animal smell coming off them.

Coming in from his left, now making plenty of noise about it, they gave him just enough warning for him to react. He unslung the sack, dumped it on the ground and stepped away fast. The one in the lead fell over it, pitching forward, a cry bursting from him, the length of lumber he had been carrying falling to the ground. The sudden fall of the first man checked the next one, but the third, an arm raised, he, too, holding a length of lumber the size of a wagon-spoke, came on in at Taber who, retreating, managed to avoid the downcoming blow. Taber lashed out with his left fist and heard the satisfying smack on the other's face and felt the pain of the blow against his own knuckles and the jolt of it up his arm.

The respite that the dropped sack and the blow had won him, however, was to be short-lived. While the man he had struck had gone swaying aside, the other two, soon recovering, now came at him. The one who had been tripped had regained his piece of lumber, and Taber, though still retreating, was caught by a blow on his left shoulder. He went sliding sideways; then, when the man, crowding closer, tried to club him again, Taber, his hat now fallen, drove forward with his head, connecting with the nose of the man in front of him. As this man yelled and pulled away, obviously hurt, Taber, using both hands, seized the length of lumber, tearing it from the other's grasp. By no means in the clear, Taber was at least armed as dangerously as were the other two.

One of them said, 'Jailbird . . . ' The air sang as club arced down dangerously but was blocked vibratingly by Taber's club. The second man came in. Taber lowered his piece of lumber, then drove it end-on at this one and caught him full in the mouth, sending him staggering backwards. Then Taber himself was hit, caught glancingly on the head an inch above the left ear and he staggered, yet instinctively lashed out. The swing of the club found no target but was enough to clear the way in front of him. With his head ringing and warm blood running, he began laying about him wildly, edging forward with each swipe until he was rewarded with heavy contact.

They left him. One moment they were there, milling, trying to avoid his furious onslaught, and the next, or so it seemed, they had put distance between themselves and him. Taber knew that one of them at least was badly injured. Man stench and whiskey stench seemed to be clinging to Taber himself. He had been hurt and was trying to draw more air into his lungs, but it was like fire in his throat. He propped himself against a stack of lumber and gradually brought his breathing under control, wearily, his left shoulder, his hands and his head paining him. He prowled around, recovered his hat and his sack of belongings. Taber slung this on his shoulder and began plodding on towards the rooming-house he was seeking.

In deep shadows a cigarette glowed. Taber stopped. Even if he had not been able to discern the gleam of a metal badge on the shirt, he would have known from the general set of the man, the largeness and roundness of face and body, that he was looking at Charon County Deputy, Aaron Cobb. Cobb spat a minute piece of tobacco from his lips. It seemed that he, too, had no doubt as to who it was who was standing before him.

'Mighta knowed there'd be a ruckus soon as yuh come, Taber.'

'The bastards were waiting,' Taber said in his grating voice. 'Where were you, Aaron?'

Cobb spun what was left of the quirly to the dirt. 'If that means what I think it means, then I take it right unkindly.' And he added the word that one of Taber's attackers had used. 'Jailbird.' Then, 'What yuh come back here for, Taber?'

Taber did not raise his voice. 'Money,' he said. 'Money that belongs to me. An' one or two other matters.'

'That so? Well, mister, I got some advice. 'Nother train through here in a coupla days. Best all 'round if yuh climb on it.'

Taber said, 'In my time I've been given plenty of advice. Most of it turned out to be this kind of shit.' He walked on past Cobb and did not look back. Taber's head was throbbing from the blow he had taken.

2

Maggie Corbin, with a long face, the skin sagging as though melting, stood staring at him. Her head was barely level with Taber's midriff. 'By God, I'll say this fer yer, yuh got a nerve. An' by the looks o' yuh, there's others that think it.'

'Sure got me a Charon welcome,' Taber said. 'But they were sweepings out of a saloon an' not up to what they were sent to do.' She stared up at him with her pouched, brown-bean eyes. No doubt she had noticed the blood coming from the side of his head. She had not said she wouldn't let him have a room, nor, as yet, said that she would.

'They didn't waste no time,' she said. She was studying him as though at some often talked about myth now suddenly become a reality. 'I rent a room to yuh, it could come back on *me*.'

'I'll not be around here long.' He was unsure if that was likely to be true. 'I've come to see Albert Stroud at the bank.'

Still she was not convinced. 'Fer some folks hereabouts, ten minutes would be too long. Cain't make up my own mind about yuh, John Taber. An' I've never understood what it is about yuh that riles Sam Stedman as much as it does.'

'The sister. Jane Reed.' There had to be more to it than that, though, which was a good part of why he was really here. Even when he added another reason he knew it was still not nearly enough to account for the enduring acrimony. 'An' Sam's likely to be looking for high office. He'd not want the likes of me anywhere near.'

'High office? Oh, he is that,' Maggie said. 'Still sees hisself as the man at the top o' the heap, Sam does.'

So that hadn't changed. Taber

hadn't expected that it would. The driving ambition of Sam Stedman; solid defender of the people's rights; owner of S-Bar, the biggest ranch in the territory; but that had never been enough for Stedman. True, it afforded him power of a sort, but he had never made a secret of his desire for political office. Working, he had so often said in his booming voice, in everybody's interests. The more cynical were inclined to see that as the interests of beef producers. A player of careful cards, Sam Stedman. People went out of their way to stay on side with the man. Even Harve Beddoes, Charon County Sheriff, while affecting independence, made sure that he stayed on good terms.

Maggie Corbin, once she saw the money — though there was not much of it to see — came to an agreement. 'But first sight o' trouble fer me an' out yuh go.' The woman went past him to the front door and looked out, as though to reassure herself that other men had not followed Taber to her establishment.

Taber nodded. There was a lot he wanted to say but could not afford to. Within the space of a dozen hours, others in and around Charon had become aware that John Taber had indeed come back. Phena Radich for one, and her son Dave. Phena's dark, faded good looks were marred by the firm clamp of her mouth. There was a likeness in the son, equally dark, good-looking, yet with a shiftiness that was all the more evident now upon hearing Taber's name. So, at first there was concern, but soon enough that look was overtaken by one of scorn.

'That man, that Taber, he come lookin' fer trouble, he'll sure enough find it.'

Phena rounded on him. 'Keep well out o' his sight, Dave! Anyways, there's plenty more in that town that'll want him gone. He'll be moved on.' Her expression said that she was less certain than she sounded.

In Charon, the squarely built, ugly, overweight man, County Sheriff Harve Beddoes, coming in off the street to find both of his deputies in the office, knew why they were there.

'Knew he was comin', an' I know he's come. What I want to know is where he's at right now.'

'Seen 'im last night, late,' Cobb said. 'Down to Maggie Corbin's.' Then, 'On the way there he had him some problems.' Beddoes stared at Cobb. So did the other deputy, Nate Cooper. This was something that Cobb had not mentioned. 'Some boys was waitin' in Leclerc's lumber yard. I come along right after.' Now Cooper was staring hard at Cobb, but said nothing. Beddoes was waiting for more. 'Last I seen of 'em,' Cobb said, 'they was in the back room at Al Meyer's.' A billiards establishment on Fremont. 'One of 'em got knocked around worse'n t'other two.'

'Names?'

Cobb shrugged. 'Drifters. Not worth

throwin' in the cage an' have the county feed 'em. My bet is they'll be gone right soon.'

Cooper asked, 'Why would drifters set on Taber? An' how'd they know he might come? An' when?'

'They wasn't what yuh might call talkative. 'Fact, one on 'em, he'll not git around to talkin' much for the next coupla months. Mouth all broke up.'

To Cooper, Beddoes said, 'Nate, I allers did tell yuh there's a whole lot o' currents runnin' hereabouts where John Taber's concerned. Cain't expect tidy answers.'

If it did not seem enough for Cooper he held back from saying so. Beddoes, as he well knew, could turn awkward real quick.

If there was a hint of tension in the county office, there was more, if held in check, between one of Charon's leading merchants, Robert Voller of the mercantile, and his wife, Emily. They were an unlikely pairing; he a man in his late fifties, balding, his clothes of good quality but shapeless, a dour man for all his success in business. Emily was at least twenty years younger, not beautiful, but good-looking, with shiny dark hair and intensely blue eyes; a neat and tidy woman, always busy, if not around the house which stood a few yards behind the mercantile building, then out and about, giving help to those she perceived as needing it. Though Charon was a town that had grown steadily, there was no doctor; or there had been, but he had turned out to be a drunk. And some druggists had been no better. So Emily, along with other women, had become skilled in treating minor injuries and simple ailments, purely as a matter of necessity, one of the consequences of living in what, essentially, was a cowtown, a place that some were inclined to observe, wryly, perhaps ought to have had its name changed to Stedmanville, such was the influence of the huge S-Bar spread. Emily's husband was on very agreeable terms with Sam Stedman and wanted to stay that way. That was the way things worked.

Robert Voller was stopped in his tracks, having heard that John Taber was indeed back in Charon. Everybody had heard rumours that the man might come, but many had chosen to dismiss them. Even now, he said, 'By God, he's stickin' his neck out. He's got a brass nerve, that man.'

Emily had no desire to get into another snappish argument. Over recent years there had been more than enough of those, and in recent months, increasingly abrasive ones. And if she had chosen to defend Taber, at least to some extent, it would be certain to cause a fierce explosion of anger from this often intractable man. For Emily, in spite of what Taber had first been accused and then convicted of, and had been sent to prison for, had never quite been able to equate that man with the one she had believed she had come to know to some extent. And to admit it, had liked. Now she left her husband still muttering about Taber and went from the mercantile to her house.

They had heard, too, that only a matter of minutes after he had got off the train, Taber had been attacked. By whom, Voller said, he had not discovered. Emily, aware of all of the background, had wondered if Sam Stedman or some of his men might have known all about that. For Stedman, when Taber had been arrested for armed robbery, had been an implacable lobbyist for giving him the longest possible sentence. The equally — as it turned out — irascible Judge Gilbert Ostermann had gone his own way. He had sent John Taber to state prison for four years. Emily found that she had been staring out of a window, yet looking at nothing.

In another part of Charon, in a back room at Meyer's Billiards Saloon, filthy, with dried blood all over his face, a man was being helped to stand up by two others, equally unkempt and dirty. He didn't want to be moved, but the bird-faced Meyer was on hand insisting that all of them get out.

'Don't give a shit where it is. All I want is yuh clear out o' this place.'

None of them were in good shape. Now they were no longer wanted in Charon. Slowly they moved out into the dry, garbage-littered yard, two supporting the other between them. Meyer had not wanted them here in the first place, but it had all been done in a rush, to get them off the streets, out of sight. Their horses were already in the yard, a sorry-looking lot, Meyer thought. They had to struggle to get the badly hurt man into the saddle. Meyer watched sourly as they departed. Saloon trash. They had looked it from the start. Not that Meyer had hired them. He was too protective of his money.

About this same time, John Taber was at the Western Bank and Loan. He was in the office of the banker, Albert Stroud. Stroud was a small, gingery-haired man in his late fifties, wearing thick-lensed eyeglasses. Slightly hump-backed, when he was sitting he seemed to have a hunched-forward attitude, as though listening intently to whoever was facing him. What he thought of Taber, was not betrayed by his expression. And what he had to say was direct and, so it appeared, completely without prejudice.

'Mr Taber, I can assure you that the funds held by this institution on your behalf are intact and available to you.' Not that the funds were substantial.

Taber nodded, then said, 'It's my guess, Mr Stroud, that some people would have come knocking at your door over that.'

Stroud's eyes seemed enlarged behind his eyeglasses. 'I have to admit, Mr Taber, that there have been some . . . overtures made to me from time to time. Needless to say, those approaches were successfully resisted by this bank.'

Though not confident of the answer he would get, Taber asked, 'Who was it, trying to get at my money?'

Pursing his lips, Stroud said, 'There was a degree of interest from . . . the parties who saw themselves as most aggrieved. Perceived compensation.'

'You mean Mrs Reed? Mostly Mrs Reed?'

The eyeglasses glinted. 'Not directly. No.'

'Sam Stedman.' It needed no confirmation from Stroud and got none. If the banker had heard of the attack on Taber — though he could scarcely have overlooked the cut on Taber's head — he made no mention of it. Nor did he by word or inference betray any personal opinion of Taber. As far as Stroud was concerned, Judge Ostermann had delivered all the judgment that was required four years ago. Stroud was a banker. His task was to take care of depositors' funds. He did, however, choose to offer some advice, which maybe meant that he *had* heard about what had happened after Taber had got off the train. Or he knew of other things which he would have regarded as imprudent to reveal.

'I advise that you draw only what you require, day to day, Mr Taber. The balance would be safer where it is.'

When Taber came out of the bank his attention was taken by a group of horsemen some fifty yards along the main street and in the act of dismounting. He would have recognized the big man in cord pants and high-collared, heavy jacket anywhere. Sam Stedman. And it was clear that the rancher had noticed and recognized Taber.

3

Taber had turned away, but it soon became clear that Sam Stedman had remounted, along with a couple of his top-hands, and all three came bobbing along the main street. They rode on beyond the walking Taber before angling their horses in towards the boardwalk. They reined in and waited for him. All were mounted on sturdy saddlers.

Stedman did not appear to be armed and maybe wasn't. The two men with him, Augie Leech and Matt Jenner, both dressed in range clothing and with tall-crowned, dusty hats, were hard-faced men. Jenner's was badly pock-marked. They were armed with pistols and, today, so was Taber, having taken shellbelt, holster and Smith & Wesson Army from his canvas sack before visiting the bank.

Without preamble, Stedman came right out with what was on his mind.

'Ain't wanted around here, jailbird.'

'I reckon you've made that point already,' Taber said.

The look on Stedman's face put the first doubt in Taber's mind, but he pushed the point anyway to see what might come out. 'Who were they, Stedman? Some whiskey-fired, out-of-work cow nurses?'

Stedman's face flushed. He was seldom spoken to in this way. Leech and Jenner sat glowering down at the man on the boardwalk. They were waiting for the merest nod from the rancher. But Stedman said, 'I got no notion what it is yuh're jawin' about, mister, but I'll give yuh fair warnin': you an' your kind ain't wanted. Best yuh git done whatever it is yuh come here for an' light out fast.' To Taber that confirmed that Stedman knew that at least one of Taber's reasons for coming was his money in Stroud's bank.

Taber said, 'I'll move on when I'm good an' ready. Made that clear last night to some third-rate hard-noses. Cobb's been given the same message. Now you an' these two roosters have got it.'

What Stedman might have said to that was not to be known, for Matt Jenner, his face aflame, nudged the horse closer and brought his quirt slicing down across Taber's right shoulder, cutting the shirt and starting a narrow welling of bright blood. When Jenner lifted his arm to do it again, however, Taber moved in underneath it fast, grabbed one side of Jenner's open leather vest with both hands and dragged the horseman towards him. As Jenner came out of the saddle, Taber jumped back. Jenner pitched heavily to the street, but his near boot had failed to come free of the stirrup. The horse whickered and tossed its head and began backing away. Taber swept his hat off, waving it. The horse reared, white-eyed and went prancing sideways, dragging Jenner. Leech and Stedman had hauled their own mounts clear. Leech's right hand dropped to the handle of the pistol he was carrying and he made to drag it free. Tabor was ahead of him, Leech now looking into the black eye of the .44 Smith & Wesson.

Stedman began roaring a general command, '*Hold up! Hold up!*'

People had stopped to watch what was happening between Taber and the S-Bar. Many now took cover in doorways. A pistol had been drawn. Taber was saying to Leech, 'Go ahead, cowboy, pull that goddamn thing . . . '

Stedman was now yelling at Leech to back off. Jenner's horse was still moving, Jenner being tugged and dragged, dust rising around man and animal.

To Stedman, Taber said loudly, 'Somebody lied, Sam. By God, somebody lied. Lied or held back. It makes no odds. If you think I'm going away, think again. An' if either o' these weasels come near me again, you'll be diggin' holes for 'em. Believe it.'

For the first time, perhaps, Stedman and anybody else who heard and saw, realized the depth of Taber's anger. His menace was suddenly there, naked and unmistakable. Yet, as suddenly as he had drawn the pistol, Taber slid it back in its holster and, with his bloodied shirt, went back on the boardwalk and walked away. He did not look back, underscoring his contempt.

The fiery stripe across his shoulder had fuelled Taber's fury. Not for one moment did he believe that what he had done to Jenner and what he had said to Sam Stedman would mark the end of the matter. Stedman was by no means the kind of man to be turned away from any purpose he had in mind. And there could be no doubt that his immediate purpose was to see John Taber gone, not only from this town but from this territory. But at least some cards had been spread on the table, face up.

Taber returned to the rooming-house and there stripped off his shirt and sponged the livid stripe across his shoulder and down his back. He dried it and then sat, bare from the waist up, on the edge of the cot. He allowed his mind to go back, beyond the years of prison, to the wild night that, eventually, had put him there.

A few miles south of Charon was a small horse ranch owned by a man named Arn Trubshawe and it had been there that Taber, seeking work, had been taken on as a general hand and a breaker of horses. Skilled at what he did, he had struck up a friendship with his employer. But, in the nature of the work they did, there were daily hazards. Taber had been slammed against a corral pole by a particularly fractious stallion and had broken his leg. It was during that time that Emily Voller had come to his awareness, for she had been giving help to an ailing doctor named Brabant.

When Taber was fit enough to climb aboard a horse, but not to put in a full day's work at Trubshawe's, he justified his presence by exercising some of the already broken horses around the ranch and along the trail between Trubshawe's and Charon. It had been along that trail on one occasion, just after sundown, that the mount he had been on went lame. An hour away from the ranch, and in rough brush country, he had assessed the seriousness of the injury to the horse and had concluded that it was treatable. He made up his mind to unsaddle the animal and picket it off the trail and walk back to Trubshawe's and from there, fetch out a high-sided wagon to pick up the horse.

Some way along the trail, however, the Shelby-Charon stage had been brought to a halt by a mounted man wearing a canvas mask with only eyeholes cut in it. The Wells Fargo messenger had been caught by surprise and was sitting alongside the driver, arms raised, under the menace of the long pistol.

Three passengers had been aboard the stage, an elderly man, a middle-aged man and a woman. Soper, the middle-aged man, might well have resisted there and then, but the road agent had wagged the pistol at him, so he and the other two had got down out of the stage, the woman helping the old man. The horseman had ordered the messenger to throw the box down.

From that point it had all started to go wrong, the Wells Fargo man, affecting to be having trouble clearing the green and white, iron-strapped box from beneath the seat. Impatient, the pistol-man had demanded money and valuables from the passengers. As it happened, none were carrying much money, but there were a couple of watches, and from the woman, a distinctive brooch set with semi-precious stones. All these articles the road agent had taken and pocketed.

The box was still not down and

it had been then that horses had been heard approaching. The bandit had been caught in two minds. Self-preservation had won the day. He had hauled his horse around and had gone spurring away. The passenger, Soper, had at once drawn a pistol from inside his coat and had fired at the fleeing bandit and had crowed in triumph, claiming that he had hit him. The stage driver had not been so sure. But before the messenger could get a shot in, the rider had vanished into the brush.

The approaching riders had turned out to be some men from Sam Stedman's S-Bar and had been particularly welcomed by the woman, Jane Reed, the widowed sister of their employer. Most of the S-Bar had headed away after the bandit, encouraged by Soper's claim to have hit him.

John Taber was in the act of stooping to release the cinches when he had become aware of a rider who was coming fast. Indeed before Taber had had time to do much more than straighten up, the horseman, riding through the gathering gloom, was almost upon him. He discarded or dropped something as he rode, but was holding a pistol. Perhaps coming suddenly upon a dismounted man had been the cause of his next action, for, as he had come near to Taber, he had fired the pistol at him, then had gone pounding on.

A searing poker of fire had whipped along Taber's left side and he had fallen to the ground. Not a deep wound, it was a painful one, and Taber had taken a few minutes to gather himself. He was already on his feet, the left side of his shirt bloodied, when he had heard the sounds of other riders, horses blowing, bit-chains clinking, the yapping voices of the men sharp in the oncoming night.

There was no way out even if he had realized that he was in some danger. They had surrounded him and his lame horse. By chance one of them had stopped and had picked up what had seemed at first to be a light-coloured cloth. It had turned out to be the canvas mask worn by the bandit.

Taber had taken his share of knocking around as they had tried to find out what he had done with the articles that the passengers had said had been stolen from them. Presently, the stage had come along and there had followed a tirade of abuse and a certain amount of confusion over the height of Taber and their impression of the bandit's height and build. But it had all been swept away in the excitement of having run the man down, a man, moreover, whose wounded side simply confirmed Soper's claim to have hit him.

So Taber was taken into Charon and even though, next day, Trubshawe had come in and had spoken for him, it had been manifestly clear that from the moment that S-Bar had surrounded him that there would be no way out for Trubshawe's ranch hand. Sam Stedman had stormed up and down in outrage. His own sister no less, had been robbed, not only of some money but of a brooch that was prized, not so much for its intrinsic value, but for the sentiment it represented. Nobody on earth treated a Stedman in that fashion and got away with it. And the mood of the populace had been in tune with the powerful rancher. Too often, at that time, had there been acts of violence committed in Charon County. Now the people sought retribution. So, in a sense, John Taber was made an example to others. No matter that they had claimed he must have hidden both money taken and the stolen articles yet they had failed to locate any. No matter that there had been lingering doubts about his general build and his demeanour when set against their fleeting impression of the man who had held up the stage: there was an inevitability about the outcome.

Yet back in Charon now, Taber knew in his very bones that somehow there had been much more to it. On the scale of felonies at that time it surely had not ranked high. No one had been shot at, much less injured. Yet there had been a determined push to have him branded as the miscreant and to have him summarily dealt with. Somewhere around here, so Taber strongly believed, lay the answer to it. And maybe the answer to who it really was who had held up the Shelby-Charon stage four years ago.

Later, after sundown, feeling the close oppression of the small room, too near in its dimensions to a prison cell, Taber slipped on a clean shirt and went out. He would visit a café, then think about what his next move might be.

Whether or not she had been watching for him he would likely never know, but after he had eaten and was passing near a shadowed corner leading off the main street, Emily Voller, wearing a blue cloak with a hood, spoke to him. At the same time he was aware of a fragrant perfume.

'I saw what happened today, John. How are you?'

4

A cold, blustery wind had sprung up. To gain shelter from it they moved a short distance along the road that branched off the main street and into the closed, awning-covered doorway of a lightless building. Emily's face was no more than a pale blur inside the hood of her cape.

'You're taking a big chance, talking with me,' Taber told her.

'Nowadays I make up my own mind about what I do, who I talk with.' He believed he could hear a note of resentment in her tone, but not towards him. It was likely that none of her past activities, caring for the sick, helping the needy, had been carried out with the uncritical approval of Robert Voller, so Taber thought. Again she said, 'I saw what happened. That S-Bar man. Sam Stedman could have prevented it. He chose to say nothing until you got the upper hand.'

'Sam's among others who don't want me anywhere near this town. This county.'

'What was it brought you back?'

'Money. There's still some of mine in Stroud's bank. Not a lot, but enough to get me started again. Stroud didn't ask questions. He didn't offer any opinions. He just told me the money was still there.'

'He seems a strange man. But I think there's more to Mr Stroud than meets the eye.'

'Yeah, a strange man but a straight one. They've been at him to get my money released. Compensation. He wouldn't budge. The court didn't make any order about it. I think Stroud was put under some pressure. He didn't buckle.'

The wind was eddying, even here, tugging at her cloak. 'So, now you know it's safe, what will you do?'

'For one thing, I'll not be trodden

underfoot by Sam Stedman or any of his boys. He's had it too easy in the past. But there's something more underneath this. After I was brought in, they couldn't get me in front of a judge fast enough. What I told the court was the truth. The man who held up the stage was the same one who shot me. They didn't find any of the things I was supposed to have taken an' God knows they spent some time looking. Maybe they think one of the things I'm about to do here is pick 'em up. But no, there's got to be more to it than that. I've had four years to think about it. Now it's my turn to look around and ask questions.'

She said, 'The driver of the stage, he's long gone. Where, I don't know. Not that he'd have been any use to you. He wasn't, back then. The messenger's dead, so I've heard. About two years ago, in Shelby. The passenger who shot at the bandit wasn't seen again. I think he was a Chicago man. The other, the old man, I don't know what happened to him, where he went.'

'Which leaves Jane Reed.'

Emily said, 'She's still living on S-Bar. She's not often seen in Charon. When she does come in, usually she's with some of Sam's men, or with Sam himself.'

She was looking at Taber intently, but it was too dark for her to read his expression. He said, 'I'll not forget Jane Reed. She's a Stedman if ever there was. I watched her all through, all the time she was giving her evidence. Never took my eyes off that woman. She didn't want to look right at me. I've thought about it damn' near every day, since. I reckon she knew it wasn't me. Or she had some real doubts.'

'Sam Stedman wouldn't ever accept that.' Then, 'According to Robert, Sam's still got his mind firmly fixed on getting into politics. He's in touch with people who already are. Well placed, some of them.'

'I thought he might've given that up. Sam's not getting any younger.'

'Not him. He'll never give up on it. Power, that's always been Sam's goal.'

Taber, glancing up and down this dark street, was still concerned about Emily being here with him. 'You can't afford to let 'em get the idea you're taking my side in this. It can't do you any good. There's not only Robert, there's all the others. I'm a pariah.'

She refused to be moved, though. 'Back then, I said I couldn't believe you'd done what they said you'd done, no matter what their testimonies seemed to show. It was all too rushed. Emotions were high. I've not changed my mind.'

'I'm grateful for that. But remember, Emily, I'm not just the accused, I'm a jailbird. I've heard the word a couple of times already.'

She asked, 'Do you plan to visit Mr Trubshawe?'

'Maybe. I doubt he'd shoot me on sight.'

'No, he'd not. I've talked with him a time or two. He still can't get over it. He doesn't believe it either. Go see him, John, when you can.'

Taber said, 'Aaron Cobb didn't lose any time offering me advice. It was the same as I got from Stedman: get out of Charon.'

'The men who set on you? You don't have any idea who they were?'

'No. To begin with, I put that right at Sam's door. I'm not so sure now. I reckon he was surprised. An' the two who were with Sam today, they weren't in the bunch that jumped me. No, somebody hired some drunks who weren't up to it.' Then he said, 'Caught sight of Phena Radich an' that wild boy of hers, Dave. They had a buckboard in town. Sure gave me the stare, Dave did. Thought he'd have left these parts, long since.'

'Phena does her best to keep a rein on him. She's still on that small place out there, just her and Dave. She still trades her produce here.'

'An' Sam Stedman, he still lets 'em be?' Why the ever-expanding S-Bar had not sought to swallow up Phena Radich's place long ago, as it had most other land-holdings throughout Charon County, had long been the stuff of discussion. 'Maybe, like Arn Trubshawe's, too small a place to be a burr under Sam's saddle,' Taber said. But certainly, Sam Stedman must have found Dave Radich, now in his mid-twenties and unendingly loud-mouthed and posturing, real hard to take. Then Taber said, 'I'd give a lot for a straight talk with Jane Reed.'

'I doubt you'll be able to manage it, unless she comes into Charon and you can speak to her when the S-Bar are elsewhere. She doesn't come often, anyway. And she'll soon enough know that you're here. Probably she does by now. If you're right in what you think, that she was never really convinced it was you at that stage, then she's got good reason to stay well clear of you.'

'I've got to at least try to see her,' Taber said.

'There is just one chance that she'll come into town. Maybe quite soon. At Abigail Hunt's shop there's a new shipment of fabrics. Most of the women in the county will want to look them over. That's one thing that would bring Jane into Charon. Nobody else out there could do it for her.'

'She's not been in yet? You're sure?'

'I'm sure. And she wasn't with Sam and his men today.'

Taber thought it was useful information, holding out a hope, a slim one maybe, that he might manage to get close to Jane Reed. 'I'll keep my eyes peeled for her.'

'You'll be taking a chance. The Stedman riders will never be far away.'

'That's a chance I'll have to take.'

'Watch out for that man Aaron Cobb, too. You say he's warned you already. He'll look for any chance at all to lay some charge on you. I don't like that man at all. I think he's devious and vindictive.'

'Yeah, I'll watch Aaron. An' Beddoes.

No doubt old Harve's still right in Sam's pocket. There's nothing that'll move anywhere in Charon County but Sam will get to hear of it from Harve.'

Emily said, 'Of the three in that county office, Nate Cooper's the only one I'd really trust. I've always thought that he's a decent man. But, of course, what Mr Beddoes says goes. Cobb's always right with Beddoes. Nate Cooper can't stand against them, even if, sometimes, he probably thinks he should.'

That was certainly true. Taber knew it. 'The cards are well stacked against me, I've got to admit that. But Emily, I can't just walk away. I didn't hold up that stage. Maybe whoever did do it is long gone. Just some drifter. But I don't think so. I can't get past the notion that somebody, somewhere in this county knows a whole lot more about it than they'll ever admit. While that's in my mind I can't leave it alone.'

'After the trial,' she said, 'after you'd

been taken away there was a strange atmosphere here. Nobody wanted to talk about what had happened. It was as though, over and done with, the whole thing had to be put firmly in the past. Young Dave Radich was the only one that I can remember who shot his mouth off around town. He was calling you all the names he could lay tongue to — until, finally, Phena told him to hold his peace. She'd had more than enough.' Emily sighed. 'Over the years Dave's worn her down. He's made that poor woman older than she is.'

'From what I recall,' Taber said, 'even Beddoes and Cobb let Dave Radich have more rein than any of the other young hellraisers.'

'I know. I've never understood why that should be,' Emily said. 'Except maybe out of some regard for Phena.' She drew a long breath. 'But none of that is going to help you find out what happened. You were in the wrong place at the wrong time, John.'

'I was, an' it cost me. Now's the

time for the payback. I can't get the four years back, no matter what. But I've served that time. They can't put me away for it twice.'

She came back to what she had said earlier. 'No, but they can look for any excuse at all to throw you in a cell.' Perhaps she had been about to ask,

'*Is it worth it?*' but at the last instant, checked herself. Instead, from some pocket underneath her cloak she brought out a small brown jar. 'Some salve. You must be in pain from the whip cut. This will help.'

'I'm real obliged, Emily. Now you'd best go.'

'Take care, John.' The briefest touch of fingers on his hand and she was gone, swallowed up in the deep shadows.

Taber waited until he was certain that she would have arrived on the main street, then a couple of minutes longer to allow her to get well clear before he, too, moved away. He went along a boardwalk on Main, head slightly down, his face for the most part shadowed by the wide-brimmed hat, until he came to the corner of the street where Maggie Corbin's rooming-house stood. His mind was still full of Emily Voller, her soft voice, all that she had said to him until her final, brief touch, leaving her faint perfume. She disturbed him as much if not more now, than she had done more than four years ago.

The lamp above Maggie Corbin's front door was lit but not shining brightly. As he approached he was overtaken by a feeling of unease, and he even slowed his pace as he neared the rooming-house. Across on the opposite side of the street stood several buildings showing no lights whatsoever. Whoever it was had been waiting for Taber to arrive. His eyes caught the merest suggestion of movement, then flame stabbed out as a pistol banged. Lead wafted past Taber's body and slammed into the front wall of the rooming-house. Taber, crouching, went crabbing across into the open street, the Smith & Wesson coming up, even as he was shot at again. This time, though, the shooting was misdirected as though the pistolman, disconcerted at not having hit Taber with the first one, now feared the answering fire that must surely come. There was the sound of boots, pounding along the dry, hard-packed street as the shooter turned tail and fled.

Taber, however, did not shoot. Instead, he set out after the man who had tried to kill him, hoping that, at some place spilled lamplight might give him away, or at least reveal the colour and kind of his clothing. Without calling or even uttering a sound, Taber ran. Pursued and pursuer, however, were now in a virtually lightless back street, around the very corner where Taber had been attacked only a matter of hours ago.

The pistolman had not gone to ground. Taber was aware of him some forty or fifty yards ahead, still running. If he continued on along this street, then at its further end he must come closer to the Charon depot, and although there was little light there — tonight no headlamp of a train — perhaps the running man would become limned against what paltry light there was.

It was not to be, however. Perhaps coming to the same conclusion, the man ahead suddenly veered right and, as Taber came pounding along the middle of the street, he realized that all else had fallen quiet. Taber stopped. He crouched, pistol still gripped in his hand. Seconds went sliding by. A minute. Another. Finally Taber came to the conclusion that his man had gone. He straightened slowly from his crouch and slid the pistol back in its holster. He made his way back along the street to the lumber yard corner and there paused. There was some activity in front of the rooming-house. He could see Maggie Corbin, two or three women and several men, one of whom was the round-bodied deputy, Aaron Cobb.

Taber came pacing towards them. A long barrel glinted as Cobb drew his pistol. 'Hold up there, mister!' Taber kept coming, walking right up to Cobb until the deputy's barrel was all but touching his belly.

'You ag'in,' said Cobb. 'Taber, yuh're gittin' to be one of our biggest problems.'

'There's a bigger problem around the streets somewhere. One that took a couple of shots at me,' said Taber. 'Not that it matters, Aaron, you'd never have caught the bastard without your horse.' Then, in a sharp, hard tone that made the small group stand quite still, Taber said, 'Uncock that thing, Deputy, or I'll take it and ram it up your fat ass.'

For a moment it seemed that Cobb, goaded beyond reason, would pull the trigger. Maybe it was someone saying, 'My God!' that gave the lawman pause.

Cobb gently uncocked the pistol and lowered it.

'Yuh'll keep, Taber. But by God, your time'll come, an' mebbe sooner than yuh think.'

5

Emily Voller's prediction came to pass within hours. As Taber was emerging from a café on Main on a morning that was as cold and blustery as the previous evening had been, he caught sight of Jane Reed. She had driven to a halt a light spring wagon drawn by a pair of strong-looking horses, had climbed down and, along with other women gathering there, was entering a store devoted to the selling of fabrics and women's goods. If S-Bar men had come in with her, none was in sight.

It had been Taber's intention to go down to the Ace Corral and Livery to hire a buckboard, but having seen the woman, he delayed, figuring that he had to take what might be the only chance he would get to speak with her. For as he had said to Emily, he was sure that there had been uncertainty about Sam Stedman's sister all through the trial. Taber had become convinced that, even if she did not hold the key to the whole affair he might be able to extract from her valuable pointers that he needed. With eyes narrowed in the cutting wind, he surveyed the main street. Dust was being driven along and a few tumbleweeds were bouncing. Signs and awnings were being buffeted and the few people who were around were walking with heads bent, holding fast to their hats.

On the opposite side of the street, the mercantile was open but at present there were no customers inside. Only Robert Voller and Emily. They could see John Taber. The dour man with thinning hair, Voller, was regarding the wind-swept street, and Taber, standing just across there in the shelter of the doorway, with displeasure that was undisguised.

'Got no business comin' back here, that man,' Voller said. 'This town don't want his kind.'

'Then why don't we empty the saloons and have their shutters put up?' Emily asked. Before he could say anything to that she answered her own question. 'I know. It must be because they turn a dollar. A dollar turns a blind eye.'

Voller gave his younger wife a sour glance, but not because of the remark and her knowledge that he had money invested in one of the saloons. His mind was still fixed on John Taber. 'Yuh took his part back then. Sounds to me like you're doin' it again.'

'It's just that I can't go along with hypocrisy.'

Voller's veined face flushed. Suddenly he gave a sharp look. 'Emily, have you seen this man? Talked with him any since he come back?' When she did not answer immediately he repeated the question. 'Have you talked with him?'

'What if I have? I treated him when he was injured. He's never made any move to harm me and it's not likely that he will.'

'By God, woman, we can't afford to have our names talked of in the same breath as John Taber's! I've said, this town don't want him. The whole damn' county don't want him. Where did you see the man? When?'

'Yesterday.'

'When, yesterday?'

'Robert I won't be cross-questioned like this.'

'*When*?'

'After dark.'

Now he was deeply angry, rounding on her. There had been moments like this in the past, when he had seemed to be on the very brink of striking her. Now, as on those other occasions, he checked himself. 'I forbid you to speak to him again!'

'If I believe that anyone, anyone at all, needs help that I can give, I'll give it. We've had all this out before, Robert. Taber was hurt. You saw what happened. He'd been whip-cut. I gave him some salve. I'd do it again, for John Taber or anybody.'

Voller turned away sharply, walked a couple of paces as though to relieve his feelings, stopped and came back. 'It's not our place — your place — to get mixed up in this, Emily.'

'What does Sam Stedman have against Taber, even now? All about the botched robbery of a stage? Because Jane was aboard and lost some trinkets? Well, I don't believe it was Taber. Maybe there are others who don't, either, but haven't the courage to say so.'

'The man had a fair trial. The evidence was too strong. He was found guilty. He was sent to jail.'

'So he's paid his dues. Or more likely, somebody else's.'

'God damn it Emily! You're still *defendin'* the man!'

'Right now I simply don't understand why he has to serve two sentences, the court's and this county's. That's what all this comes down to.'

Across the windy street, Jane Reed, her cloak flapping, had come out of the store. Taber was moving towards her. The woman did not notice him until he had got within a yard of her. She had been stowing some packages in the wagon. When she turned and saw him, her face drained of colour. Perhaps she might have expected to see him at some time, but not as soon as this and not at close quarters. Taber could see the sudden shock reflected in her eyes. A tall woman, as all Stedmans were, she was in her late thirties and had a pleasant rather than good-looking face, dark hair and dark eyes.

Taber said, 'All I ask you to do is hear me out.'

Recovering, there was now a glimpse of the Stedman confidence. 'I've got nothing at all to say to you, Mr Taber.'

'There'd be no harm hearing what I've got to say. I reckon you know that I got a bad deal. I watched you all the time you were giving your evidence. It was all supporting what others said.

You weren't sure. All I want is to hear you say it.'

'Mr Taber, you were found to be along that trail, not far from where the stage was stopped. Maybe a mile and a half. The mask was picked up near where you were. A passenger shot at the robber. You'd been slightly wounded. Recently. There was a fair trial in front of a judge whose probity is without question. Don't come back here whining to me about it now.'

He had expected resistance. What he had got was a mounting aggression. Now, this was more in keeping with a Stedman. Yet, having started, he pressed on.

'Why don't you tell me straight out if you believed it?' He had taken an involuntary half-pace closer to her. Abruptly she turned away and climbed up on the wagon. But as she did so he felt sure he had noticed a momentary hesitation, almost a weakening of resolve.

Two riders now came walking their

61

horses around a corner some thirty yards away, ducking their heads in the face of windblown dust. Sam Stedman and one of his tophands, Augie Leech. Taber stepped well back, releasing the hammer-thong as he did so. Jane Reed shook the reins, spoke to the horses and the creaking wagon moved away. Eventually Stedman and Leech followed it. Both went bobbing by. Only when wagon and riders had disappeared into the rolling dust did Taber continue on his way to the livery.

Not long after, mounted on a solid-looking black horse, Taber rode steadily out of Charon, along the trail to the south-west. Behind windows, eyes observed his departure. No doubt there would spring up speculation about whether or not he was leaving Charon for good or merely setting out somewhere for some specific purpose. Taber himself, had he been aware, and of a mind, could have told them that his purpose was not specific, no more than a desire to examine the country all along that south-western trail, to see again the place where S-Bar had come upon him, then to ride on further, to where the stage had been brought to a halt by the lone bandit. He wanted to refresh his mind about that entire area, to think about where he himself had been and had been said to be, at the time. To set the scene again, to allow his mind to go poking around among all the words, the statements, the half-truths and guesses and outright lies, all in the vague, perhaps absurd hope that something, or someone, somewhere, might give him some answers he needed. Though he had met with a rebuff from Jane Reed he had by no means given up hope of approaching her again. Now more than ever did he see her as the means of taking a step towards finding out the truth. He would have to persist along that line, though in doing so would risk the wrath of Sam Stedman. Indeed, he would be risking swift retribution from

Stedman's ranchhands, after his rough handling of the top-hand, Jenner. S-Bar was not accustomed to being resisted, have others stand up to them, and they were likely to want to square matters, as they would see it, as soon as possible.

The further he rode the rougher the trail became, brush almost choking it in places; for there were no stages using this route any more. The Western Trans-Territory had consigned them to history. So it was not surprising that Taber almost rode on by the spot where, four years earlier, the horse had gone lame and the man who had held up the stage had come pounding suddenly through the gloom. For all those years, Taber had held that image in his mind, the horse, the rider, the set of him, the flare and blast of his pistol and the fire-rod that had come bursting across Taber's side. Yesterday, he had taken a good long look at Augie Leech. The way he sat his horse. Taber, however, was far from sure about that. He rode on.

Presently he arrived at the place where they said the stage had been stopped. Here, again, the brush obviously had thickened during intervening years. But even then there must have been plenty of cover for the bandit to wait and then get total surprise. That was what they had said. Suddenly the road agent was there with his pistol. Slowly Taber turned and rode back the way he had come, eventually arriving again at the place where he had been wounded and then taken.

He rode on, pondering on where the fleeing bandit might have departed from the trail, for it seemed unlikely that he would have continued on and come anywhere even close to Charon. About a quarter of a mile on, he drew the black to a halt. To his left was the beginning of a side-trail, one that was barely discernible, so little had it been used. Taber was thoughtful, realizing that it lay in the direction of Mavor Creek. He kneed the black, and with freshening interest, moved off down that trail, passing often between clumps of tall brush and lichen-covered boulders, knowing where it would lead him, thinking that there were things he ought to have remembered before this. Things that ought to have been raised at the time, four years back.

Taber came within sight of Mavor Creek. It was a sorry-looking waterway lined with brush and stunted trees, but of more interest to him, it was a place where a number of soddies had been built many years ago. The original occupants had gone long since and, over the years, their places had become shelters for all manner of people; drifters, homeless families, people of all sorts down on their luck. Always wary of strangers and particularly wary of the county law, the denizens of the soddies had become a small, remote, self-contained little community, drawn together in adversity for mutual protection; men, women, children, unkempt, and much of the time ill-fed. And almost always ill-tempered with strangers. This was an uncomfortable, miserable existence.

Yet the thought had come to Taber that maybe this was the place the bandit had come to. Maybe risking showing himself to the men here, for information about him could have been sold to great advantage. Or perhaps to be given what food could be spared and what shelter there was, by someone who knew him. Or by the entire group, who might have known him and feared him. He could have holed up in brush within sight of the soddies until such time as he felt it was safe to move in.

Smoke was rising from some of these shelters. A few people were around to watch unblinkingly as the man on the black horse approached. Come out of nowhere. Men who were suspicious as a matter of course, women with sunken eyes, children dirty, clinging to faded skirts. Taber drew the horse to a stop.

Other men and women came out of soddies. A dark-haired young woman, maybe nineteen years old, gave the horseman a sidelong look and a smile that could not be mistaken in its meaning. A very pretty, clear-skinned female, she might have spoken to him had not three or four of the men broken away and approached the horseman. Two were armed, one with a rifle of some vintage, another with a two-barrelled shotgun. Another man in this group said to the girl, 'Go back in, Nell, he ain't fer you.' The girl took no notice, still smiling faintly at Taber.

The rifleman asked, 'Who the hell are yuh, mister? What yuh want with us?'

'Passing through,' said Taber.

'Asked your name,' the other said. He lifted the rifle slightly. The shotgun that the second man had was of the kind with dual hammers, and first one, then the other, was clicked back.

'My name's John Taber.'

They were all staring at him. Then the rifleman said, 'Yuh just ain't welcome here, Taber. Sam Stedman, he gits wind that yuh come here, he might git to thinkin' we're in cahoots with yuh. He'd have these here soddies tore down. So git movin', mister.'

Taber said, 'I'm not here looking for shelter. I reckon you might have information that I need — '

The shotgunner lifted the weapon and snugged the butt-plate into his shoulder. 'One thing about these here hammer guns,' he said, 'they give a man a fair sightin'.'

Taber realized that these men were not bluffing. He was now a whisker away from being blown out of the saddle. He could be buried out in the brush and nobody the wiser. He did not argue. He nodded, lifted his gloved hands slightly and turned the black around. He kept the black down to a walk, as he had done when he had ridden in here. But all the way out, until he knew that he would be screened from them by brush, his skin crawled and he found that he was sweating profusely. He had certainly not expected to be welcomed at that place, but the rebuff that he had got had been harsh and immediate. It sure underscored the influence that the rancher, Stedman, had, even in such a poverty-stricken place, people there with only those rude shelters to lose.

About an hour later he was in a yard, an area of hardpack in the middle of several corrals in which numerous horses were moving, and at one end of which was a split-log ranch house with a low-pitched roof. There were some outbuildings too, and a high barn. Trubshawe's.

The white-whiskered man wearing Levis and a blue and white check shirt and an old, high-crowned hat, came out of the barn, screwing up his eyes until he had recognized the rider.

'By God,' Trubshawe said, 'didn't think to see yuh in these parts ag'in, John.'

'Nobody else did either,' Taber said. 'Some of 'em have said so. An' a few of 'em have left me in no doubt at all.' He swung down and hitched the horse. 'I'll not stay long,' he said. 'Been taking a look around, down the old trail. Got turned away from the soddies along Mavor Creek before I could spit. They're sure a jumpy bunch down there.'

'Stedman,' Trubshawe said. 'Still the same as ever it was. Nobody in this county wants to risk gittin' on the wrong side o' Sam. Or on the wrong side o' some o' his boys. Everything yuh touch, everything yuh do, Sam's hand turns out to be in it somewheres. Never be settled in his mind 'til he's runnin' the whole shebang.' Trubshawe looked somewhat shamefaced. 'Cain't claim I don't stay out o' Sam's way these days, John. Things is a bit tight an' I don't want to rile the man. It could turn awkward.'

With a slight grin, Taber said, 'If you don't mention I called then I won't.' He told Trubshawe what had happened in the short time that had elapsed since he had stepped off the

Western Trans-Territory. 'About the only one in Charon who'll give me as much as the time of day is Emily Voller. An' banker Stroud.' Then he told the old horse rancher what was in his mind and why, apart from recovering his money, he had come back here at all.

Trubshawe squinted at him. 'Yuh know already I never did believe it, John. But with things like they were, there wasn't nothin' a man could do ag'in that crowd. Right from the start, it looked bad fer yuh. No defence, out there on your own. Nothin'.'

Taber nodded sombrely. 'But somebody knows. I'm goddamn' sure of it.' He unhitched the horse and remounted. He was walking the black out of the yard but drew rein again and cast a glance back at Trubshawe. 'If it comes to it, Arn, stay well clear. Don't go getting yourself in a corner on my account. Maybe this is something I can't win.'

A mile outside Charon, moving

through thick brush, Taber, out of the corner of an eye, caught the glint of something and instinctively went plunging sideways; the horse spooked, Taber getting free of the stirrups to go thumping to the ground even as a rifle shot lashed and heavy lead went slashing through brush. It passed so close that he felt the waft of it. Rolling through lacerating branches, trying to unthong the pistol, he was aware of a horse close by. But it was going further away. His hired black was among the brush somewhere, whickering.

Dazed, Taber came up on to his knees. He had now got the pistol free but he knew that it was far too late. Unsteadily, he got to his feet. He had hit the ground hard. His left shoulder was paining him. The sound of the hard-running horse was diminishing. Taber began walking among the tall brush towards the sounds the black was making.

6

Dave Radich had ridden into Charon and he had been on the coffin varnish. Having no doubt got together some money from casual work here and there, he was doing what he most often did in those circumstances, unloading it into the coffers of Charon's less salubrious saloons. One of the grimier ones was the Red Deuce, and Dave was in there now, and he was in good voice.

'This here Taber, I reckon he ain't up to much.'

Somebody muttered, 'Then yuh'd best git the word to Matt Jenner.'

Loudly, Radich said, 'That there was luck. Next time, somebody's gonna blow Taber's lamp right out. You watch an' see.' He called for another shot. 'No, this Taber's a feller that in his own lights cain't do no wrong.

Jailbird. An' now he's got the brass nerve to come right back here, pokin' around all over.'

'Yuh seen 'im Dave? Pokin' around?'

Dave gave the man a foxy look. 'I git around. I hear things.'

But by and large the few idle men sitting around at tables in the saloon, some scuffing sawdust with their boots, chose not to say much. When young Radich was in town and on the redeye, and when he began shooting his mouth off and looking around for challengers to his opinions it was best not to risk provoking him. Since the age of fifteen or so, he had developed a reputation locally for wildness. There had been numerous unsavoury incidents in the town and others at cow camps where Dave had been, albeit temporarily, a hired hand, and he had been marked out as a braggart. But a dangerous one. He was unpredictable and had from time to time done damage to premises. Without reason he might start loosing off a pistol or set up to do some target shooting with his Winchester too close to town buildings for comfort.

Now Dave Radich was twenty-two years old, and while he still lived with his mother, Phena, on her small farm not far out of Charon, he came and went as he pleased. Dave, as he was inclined to say to all and sundry, was beholden to nobody. It was surprising to many that county sheriff, Harve Beddoes, while having given out numerous warnings about behaviour, had shown a reluctance to bear down hard on Radich. Even more surprising was that Deputy Aaron Cobb had been inclined to treat Radich's excesses lightly. Maybe, so some people opined, the officers thought well of Phena and did not want to upset her unduly.

Sam Stedman was another who seemed not to want to push Dave. Now, that sure was unusual. It was even the more so when it was recalled that there had been more than one drunken skirmish involving S-Bar hands, not only at range camps but elsewhere.

While there had been no pistols drawn, a time or two it had come close, and on at least one occasion that had been averted only through intervention by Sam Stedman himself. The hot-headed Dave Radich seemed to be living a charmed life, but there were plenty in the county who reckoned that sooner or later, Dave's luck was going to run out all on the same day.

Moving back and forth behind their clusters of china beer-pulls, the bar-dogs in the Red Deuce were regarding Dave sombrely. With an ounce of luck he would soon tire of the Deuce, particularly if he was not able to start an argument, and would move on somewhere else. Let it be soon.

Aaron Cobb must have got wind of the fact that Radich was in one of the saloons, for briefly his round face appeared over the top of the batwing doors. The deputy stood watching for no more than a few seconds, however, before moving on without uttering a word. The drinkers and card players at the tables exchanged enigmatic glances.

Later in the day, though still stiff from his dive out of the saddle and sore from brush-rakes, Taber was deep inside the S-Bar rangeland. He was moving steadily but unhurriedly. He knew that this was a long chance that he was about to take, but the clear recollection of that look of uncertainty on Jane Reed's face, right at the finish, was still in the forefront of his mind. The strong notion that the woman did indeed have doubts had caused him to push his luck in the way he was doing now. Indeed, it was a big risk he was taking, but after accosting her in town, he doubted that she would put in another appearance there until she had been assured that Taber had gone, or had been dealt with. Today the unknown rifleman out in the brushlands had come within a whisper of killing him. Next time there might be no glimmer of warning.

The day was about done when Taber came within sight of the lights that told him he was close to the ranch buildings. So far his luck had been in. He had encountered no one, nor had he heard anyone nearby.

In Charon, Dave Radich had left the Red Deuce behind him and somewhat clumsily had mounted a dusty bay horse outside. Walking the bay up the main street he bawled out greetings to anyone who caught his eye, and from time to time yelled for John Taber to come out from wherever he was hiding. Nearing the top end of the street, Radich unscabbarded his rifle and loosed off three shots into the air. As he came near the office of the county sheriff, he called out to Cobb who was standing in the doorway.

'Yuh know what, Aaron? I reckon that four-flusher, Taber, he's done lit out! Mebbe he's heard I was a-comin'!'

Cobb did not answer. But if the deputy was content in thinking that Dave Radich, having had a few hours in town was now heading home, that proved not to be the case. But this did not become apparent until some little while later.

Out on the S-Bar, Taber had come to a stop. Around the ranch buildings there were comings and goings. The cookhouse was well lit, its pipe chimney smoking into the near-night sky. Buildings and men were now no more than dim shadows. Taber's plan was to wait until the hands had gone inside the cookhouse, then circle the buildings and eventually approach the ranch house on its opposite side, away from the yard.

Then Taber slowly turned his head. From somewhere in the dusk behind him, some horsemen were approaching. There was no immediate cover to be had. Taber knew he had no option but to sit still where he was and allow the riders to go by, hoping that he would not be noticed. They were about fifty yards across to his right, mounted on walking cow-ponies. Range men coming in. Five of them. He waited. They were past him, though they had angled closer to where he was. Then one of them must have glanced back and said something to the others, for now all drew rein.

One of them called, 'That you, Bart?'

Taber walked the horse around and away from them. Someone shouted. He took no heed. Again there came a yell. Taber nudged the black horse to a trot. Suddenly a pistol banged. Taber thought the shot had been fired into the air. He increased the pace of the black. Behind him there were further shouts. Taber now clapped spurs to the horse and fled.

There was a chase of sorts, but the cow ponies were no match for the strong saddler under Taber. One further pistol shot split the air, but it was no more than a forlorn hope that the night rider would be hit. As fast as he dared, Taber crossed the rolling rangeland, heading in the general direction of Charon. His attempt to get close to Jane Reed had been a total failure. All he could be satisfied about was that it was unlikely that he had been identified by the S-Bar riders.

Taber came back into Charon at about nine o'clock and headed directly for the livery from which he had got the horse. From there he went to a café. Then he headed for Maggie Corbin's. He did not know that Beddoes had been active, looking all over for Dave Radich, and that Phena Raditch had been helping him. Or that the Vollers had heard about Radich's loud boasting concerning John Taber. Emily, indeed, had been so concerned that she had gone out in front of the mercantile, wondering if by chance she might catch sight of Taber, should he reappear. She was worried and looked it. John Taber's welfare was of greater concern to her than she would ever have dared admit. Aaron Cobb, pausing in shadows nearby, noticed her. Then he saw Robert Voller appear at the front door of the mercantile and say something to his wife that Cobb could not hear. There followed what appeared to Cobb to be an argument until Emily, with one last glance along the street, followed her husband inside.

Elsewhere, Sheriff Beddoes was saying to Phena Radich, 'Yuh got to git a halter on Dave, one way or t'other. Soon as that boy gits liquored up he starts shootin' his mouth off all over. An' then he starts shootin' the firearm off, an' that's a whole lot worse.'

Phena said, 'He's taken ag'in John Taber.' She looked worn and very tired. 'Once he takes ag'in somebody, I cain't no ways manage him.'

Inside the mercantile, the door of which was now closed and bolted, the lamps had been turned down. Emily was showing her own discontent in the face of Robert's anger. 'You and Sam Stedman. There's something going on, Robert. I want to know, now, what it is.'

'None of your concern, Emily. The merchants here, they ain't no ways pleased about this Taber comin' back. That's the man yuh seem to want to defend. Help, even, goddamn it! I'll not stand still fer that!'

'Stedman won't, is what you mean.' Anger had lent her boldness.

'Sam? Sam's concerned about this entire county. Sam, he's headed fer big things. Mark what I say.'

'If you say so. I don't care. And Mr Beddoes, he does nothing about that Dave Radich. In drink, Dave's capable of anything. And why isn't your Sam Stedman concerned about Dave's carryings on, if he's as civic minded as you claim? It doesn't add up, Robert. Nothing you've said or can say will explain it. John Taber's served his sentence. And I've said before, maybe served somebody else's sentence. There's no more that can be done to him.'

That was not quite what Harve Beddoes was saying to Phena Radich. 'We got to find Dave, an' real soon. If'n he's got some fool notion o' callin' Taber, he's gonna git in the way here.' Then he added, 'Wouldn't be at all surprised if there's others that's fixin' to solve the problem o' this here jailbird.' It was not clear whether or not Beddoes was saying he knew — certainly Phena Radich didn't — that this solution to what was seen as the problem of John Taber had, earlier on this same night, got off the train and had quickly walked around to a rooming-house on Miller. His name was Josiah Gaul.

When Taber, tired and dispirited, came within sight of Maggie Corbin's it was to see a gangly figure come walking, none too steadily, out of shadows on the other side of the street. Wherever Dave Radich had been, he had now reappeared.

'Taber, yuh bastard, I'm here to call yuh!'

Taber stopped. He recognized who it was at once. As far as he could see, no pistol had been drawn.

'I've got no quarrel with you, Dave.'

'Well, it don't matter. I got one with you, Taber.' His words were slurred. 'Yuh been give the word yuh ain't wanted here. Yuh ain't been listenin'. Now the talk's all done an' I'm here to make it stick.'

'Dave, I don't want to have to kill you.'

Radich laughed. He staggered a little. 'Big talk, jailbird. Full o' talk, that's all. Yuh don't — '

It was cut off short as someone who had walked up behind Radich made a move. There was a solid clumping sound as the barrel of a pistol was laid hard across the back of his hat. Radich gave a grunt and fell to his knees. His hat fell off. Aaron Cobb, now holstering his pistol, said, 'Taber, git off'n the street. Dave, he's gonna rest up some. But by God, mister, the trouble yuh're causin' here ain't gonna be tol'rated.'

Taber walked on and entered the rooming-house.

In a room, elsewhere, where Josiah Gaul was, the lamps had been turned almost all the way down. Men stood in shadows. Gaul had asked the name of the man he had been brought in to kill. Low-voiced, one of them said, 'John Taber.'

There was a silence. Gaul then asked, 'What do yuh know about the man?'

He was told all that they knew. Gaul listened. When he spoke again it was to the point. 'The money that was put up, it ain't enough.'

'It was agreed on.'

'It was agreed for me to come in an' take care o' some goddamn' burr under some saddles. Clean an' quick. No questions. The law to stand off.'

'Nothin's changed.'

'What's changed is who he turns out to be.'

'Yuh know Taber?'

Gaul shook his head. 'The man I know ain't John Taber. He's a feller called John Taber Rolt.'

7

Whatever became of Dave Radich after he came more or less to his senses, wasn't known, for this time he did quit Charon. But when Phena, on her buckboard, got back to the farm, expecting him either to be there or to arrive quite soon, her son was nowhere to be found, and did not come. Humiliated by both John Taber and Aaron Cobb, and no doubt with a strongly throbbing head, perhaps he had crept away into the brush to recover, like a sick animal.

The Vollers had ceased arguing, but there was a chilling bitterness in the silence that followed it. Robert Voller had closed the mercantile and had gone off to a meeting with other Charon merchants. The reason he had not specified.

Emily waited until he was out of the

way before she, too, put on her cloak and left the house. Earlier, a man who had come knocking for Robert and whom she had not been able to see, had brought news. So much, Emily had unashamedly overheard. A man had come in on the train, looking for Taber. A man named Gaul. Now, having abandoned all caution, she was standing beneath the lamp outside the front door of the rooming-house, facing Maggie Corbin.

Immediately and pointedly, Maggie said, 'We don't 'llow female visitors, Miz Voller.'

Her face colouring as much from annoyance as from embarrassment, Emily said, 'Will you please tell Mr Taber I'm here?'

Maggie gave the woman at the door a long look. At first, it seemed that she might refuse, then she turned and went scuffing away along the hall. Presently, Taber came. He stepped outside and they moved out of the lamplight.

Taber said, 'If I know old Maggie

she'll have this all around town in quick time.'

'It can't be helped. John, there's a man in Charon who's just arrived. I don't know where he is right now, but I've heard he's come looking for you.' And she told him how she had come by the information.

Taber stood quite still, looking down at her. 'Do you know what his name is?'

'Gaul. I think it was Gaul.'

He said nothing immediately. Then, 'Josiah Gaul.'

'You know him?' She saw him nod.

He said, 'It's not taken 'em long, I'll give 'em that. Telegraph, I'd say. He's come some distance.'

'He was brought here? Who would bring him?' She saw him shrug.

'Take your pick. Stedman. The town merchants. A few. Or all of 'em.' It drew no protest from her. Perhaps she suspected it too. 'Others that I don't even know about. But listen to me, Emily. The man that Gaul's been

90

brought in for, isn't John Taber. He's been brought in for John Taber Rolt.'

'I don't follow.'

'When I came through this part of the country it wasn't by chance. It was to make a fresh start a long way from where I'd been. As John Taber. That's who I am now an' who I intend to stay.' And, as though to reassure her, 'There's no dodger out anywhere for Rolt. But there's too many men like Josiah Gaul who'd come to J.T. Rolt like moths to a candle. If they're offered enough enticement.'

'What will you do?'

'Do? Nothing. Wait. Josiah, he'll have to make the first move. I'll not turn tail, either. He can call me an' take his chances, or he can leave. Josiah, he's a skilled man but he's not a fool. Maybe he didn't know exactly who it was they wanted rid of until he got here.'

'It would have made a difference?'

'It might have.'

After Emily had left, Taber returned

to his room and gave the matter of Josiah Gaul a good deal of thought. It was a bold throw of the dice by somebody — somebody who badly wanted Taber dealt with, and quickly. It served to strengthen his belief that there was indeed something to be discovered. That the man who had held up the Shelby-Charon stage had been no drifter. He had belonged in this county, this town, perhaps. And he was still here.

The following morning Taber came face to face with Josiah Gaul. A narrow-faced man with small eyes that were close together, a nose that was sharp and prominent, black hair that was bunched thickly at his neck. When Taber walked inside a café, Gaul was already sitting there. He was wearing narrow-legged brown pants, a dark-blue shirt and was slung with a pistol. If he was surprised to see Taber walk in he gave no outward sign of it. Taber, for his part, evinced none either, and took a seat at a nearby table. A plump woman came. Taber ordered breakfast.

'Heard you were here, Josiah. You're up an' about in good time.'

'Allers held that it pays to be,' Gaul said. 'Gives a man a chance to see who's around.'

They might have been no more than well-disposed acquaintances meeting by chance after a long interval. Taber observed the other man calmly, then said, 'I already know what brought you all this way.'

Chewing on thick bacon, Gaul shook his head and swallowed. He drank some coffee. 'I'da been surprised if yuh hadn't heard, John, the way things usually are.' Then he fixed Taber with an almost mischievous look. 'Come seekin' some asshole with no name. Turned out it was a John Taber. He turned out to be John T. Rolt.'

'Rolt. Taber. Plain old John. What you see is what's always been there.'

'Now,' Gaul said, wiping his plate with a chunk of bread, 'I jes' do wonder how that could be, John? Been a long time. An' I hear yuh jes' finished four years in the big cage. Things ain't been goin' too good fer yuh.'

'It can be dangerous to put money on things you get told, Josiah. This bunch here didn't even get a man's name right. People make mistakes.' He was trying to hold the other man's eye, but Gaul was concentrating on finishing his meal. Taber's own breakfast arrived.

'Reckon it's got to be like they say, John. Stands to reason. A man can git kinda . . . out o' practice.' Again he said, 'Stands to reason.'

'If it should turn out you're right, Josiah, you won't need to buy the drinks for a month. If it turns out you're wrong, well, you'll never have to worry about anything any more.'

Gaul drank the last of his coffee. When he glanced at Taber, just as he scraped his chair back and stood up, Taber believed that he glimpsed what he had been looking for. The merest flicker of doubt in the other man's eyes. Yet if it had been there, it had gone as Gaul stepped to a peg and took down his hat.

'No doubt we'll meet again,' Gaul said.

'Where?'

'Aw, you jes' go about whatever business yuh got, John. By an' by, we'll meet up. Yuh know I never was a man to rush things that had to be done jes' right.'

'Don't leave it too long, Josiah. One more thing: I'll not be the one to call it. Whoever it was brought you, they'd want that. So you call me or you up an' leave. One or the other.'

Pausing at the door, Gaul said, 'Allers did have a brass nerve, John, as I recall.' He went out, the door rattling shut behind him.

When Taber came out of the café there was no sign of Gaul. But Taber came in for some curious looks from passers-by. The word, it was clear, had spread. There was a lot more to the man they had known as Taber than anybody had imagined. It was both interesting and unsettling. On a street corner Beddoes came up to him.

'A word, Taber. Or Rolt. Or whatever your goddamn' handle is. I hear tell there's some pistolman in town. Name o' Gaul. The word is there's bad blood betwixt yuh.'

Taber shook his head slowly. 'Not bad blood, Harve. Just had breakfast with the man. All there is between us is the price some bastard paid to bring him here. For Josiah, it's only a matter of business; for me, it's a matter of no account. He's second rate, Harve. Sooner or later, in his line of work, that's fatal.'

Beddoes stood blinking his little eyes. 'I'll not have pistols fired off around these streets, mister. Take fair warnin'. Best thing yuh can do is ride out. Wherever yuh go, this Gaul, he'll no doubt foller. That way I'll git shut o' both.'

'I'm going nowhere, Beddoes. Settle that in your mind now. Go talk with whoever it was fetched the bastard. But

I'll tell you this: I'll defend myself if I'm pushed to it. If that has to be with this' — he tapped the handle of the Smith & Wesson — 'then so be it.'

Beddoes, however, though momentarily taken aback, was immovable. 'Do that, an' yuh'll be askin' to git put in the cage. By God, I'll do it!'

'Then we might well meet again,' Taber said, 'unless you can persuade ol' Josiah otherwise.' Taber walked on by. The street was very quiet. Yesterday's blustery wind had died out. There was now an almost breathless hush about the whole place. Taber noticed Robert Voller watching him from the opposite side of the street. Taber ignored him and went back to the rooming-house.

In her kitchen, Emily Voller was thinking not only about Taber but about Jane Reed, remembering what Taber had said about her. While Emily had never been close to Sam Stedman's sister, they had been on agreeable terms whenever they happened to meet. Emily had never quite been able to make up her mind about Jane Reed. Widowed, come back to what had been her home before her marriage, the S-Bar spread, she exhibited all the hallmarks of the Stedmans. Much of that had to do with her looks. Physically, she was taller than most other women, certainly much taller than Emily herself. She had the dark looks of the Stedmans, a handsomeness and, so some people insisted, their arrogance. Yet this had been something that Emily herself had never experienced in all her exchanges with the woman. On the contrary, she had found her, if anything, somewhat hesitant. And indeed there had seemed to be, at times, another quality, a certain warmth. More warmth than her brother would ever be capable of showing towards anyone. And so, no matching sense of ruthlessness. Emily had maybe seen a part of what John Taber had thought he had seen, if only for an instant. Now

Emily was beginning to think seriously about Jane.

Phena Radich, too, had a restless mind. Her son still had not come home. Mounted on a plodding farm horse she had ranged all around her property, seeking any sign of him. True, he had been absent at other times, sometimes for weeks on end, but on this occasion, as she had found out, there had been all that posturing and boasting around the Charon saloons, all that loud talking against Taber, then the confrontation with the man. That, thank God, had ended abruptly when Aaron Cobb had stepped in and buffaloed Dave.

An hour ago, Phena had crossed onto S-Bar range and she had not been long on that place before she encountered a couple of cowhands who, having sighted her from a distance, had come spurring to find out who the slow rider was. If they had been surprised to discover that it was Phena Radich, then with the reticence of their kind they had not gone as far as saying so. Nor had they demurred when she had asked them to take a message to their employer. He was to be told that she needed his help. If they had thought that such a message was unlikely to produce a result, then they would have been wrong.

Within three hours, Sam Stedman came walking his powerful roan into the small farmyard, scattering chickens, and this time the S-Bar rancher had no hard-men at his back. He got down and led the horse forward as Phena came to the yard door. Stedman, as it happened, had been about to head off elsewhere on business of his own, but he had not ignored the call from this farm woman.

In Charon, the windless calm prevailed. Yet beneath the surface of the town, tension was building. There would have been no one in that place who was not aware by now of the presence of a pistolman. Josiah Gaul, who had come for the sole purpose of seeking out the man known as John Taber. Yet time was sliding by. Hours had passed with no sign whatsoever of either man. People going about essential affairs were tending to glance up and down whichever street they happened to be on, as though nervous of a sudden outbreak of violence.

8

Some of Stedman's riders were in town, not many, but among them Augie Leech and the pock-marked Matt Jenner, the latter moving stiffly as a result of his brush with Taber. Sam Stedman himself, however, was nowhere to be seen.

The tense atmosphere that was abroad, and now the appearance of some of the S-Bar, was sufficient to draw out of the county building all three badged officers, Beddoes, Cobb and Cooper. As though to play down their presence on the streets, however, they had chosen to move around singly and with an air of casualness that was no doubt intended to belie their purpose. Yet so far Josiah Gaul had not shown himself. Neither had John Taber.

Robert Voller kept putting in an

appearance behind the long window of the mercantile, looking a mite anxious. Once he came out and had a word or two with the ambling Beddoes, but Voller did not remain long on the boardwalk after Beddoes had gone on.

Al Meyer, his grimy billiards establishment empty, was brooming away the detritus of the previous day and night. He was far from pleased. So far, on this day, no one had even come near the place. All this uncertainty brought about by the reappearance of Taber was no damn good for business and the sooner the law got on top of it the better. The stinking itinerants who had taken shelter in Meyer's back room were, of course, long gone. Gone, too, was the sore-headed Dave Radich who had also been brought to that same place after the calling of Taber nonsense and the subsequent whack over the head by Cobb, there to recover what senses Dave had even at the best of times. Where Dave Radich might be now, however, Meyer had no idea.

And he did not care, as long as that loud-mouthed, unpredictable fool was no longer sheltering under his roof. Why the raving idiot had not been thrown into one of the county cells, Meyer did not know, though he had puzzled over it. The impression that had formed in his mind was that someone, somewhere, must have spoken up for Radich on the grounds that he scarcely warranted the cost of a night's lodging at the county's expense. And when all was said and done, it came back to this: it was Taber, or Rolt as they were now calling him, that the town wanted shut of. Dave Radich seemed of much smaller consequence by comparison.

At Maggie Corbin's rooming-house Taber was making preparations to go out. He had had more than enough of the musty, poky room, and anyway, he had personal matters to attend to. With money from the bank, the first thing he intended doing was visiting the Ace Corral and Livery to make a bid for the purchase of the horse he had hired from there yesterday, together with a complete rig. When, eventually, he quit Charon, he was determined that it would not be on a train. He wanted to go in his own way in his own time. But he was not nearly ready to go yet. The things he had come here to uncover were still hidden right here, so he believed. His determination to find out the truth had strengthened even in the past few hours. Yet now that he had become known as J.T. Rolt it was inevitable that interest in him would be revived elsewhere, so he would not have unlimited time at his disposal. If he took too long, then as time went by, other Josiah Gauls would come. That thought prompted him to wonder where Gaul was right now and what might be going through the man's mind. Others might have begun to think that Taber's failure to put in an appearance so far today was out of fear at what was facing him. Gaul would know otherwise. And it would be eating at him.

Taber went along the hall and opened the front door and went out. Though he had not turned to look, he knew that Maggie Corbin, a woman seldom at a loss for something to say, had stepped into the doorway of another room and watched the tall figure departing.

Across on the opposite side of the street, Deputy Nate Cooper was leaning in the doorway of an abandoned building. Taber nodded and went strolling across to him. Cooper did not even straighten from his casual posture but nodded in return. A man in his middle thirties, of somewhat serious mien, he had not struck Taber as being anything like the other deputy, Aaron Cobb. Indeed, Cooper's manner was the very opposite of Cobb's, and reflected Emily Voller's opinion of him.

Speaking in what was a slight Southern drawl, he said, 'I'm standin' here because this is where I've been put.'

Taber gave the deputy a wry grin. 'Your boss, Beddoes, gave me the hard word yesterday. But I can't wait around all day for Josiah to make his move.' Taber stared at Cooper. 'I don't know what you've heard or what you've been told, Nate, but he didn't just happen to come here; he was brought.'

'Does Gaul admit that?'

'No. Nobody admits anything, but there've been a whole lot of comings and goings, so I believe. Maybe I'll never get to know whose money it was fetched him. Anyway, I can't allow him to pick me off. Everything on his terms. We'll have to have it out.' Then, 'I'll say it again, for what it's worth. Whoever hit that stage four years back, it wasn't me. If it had been, I'd have got my money out of Stroud's bank an' moved on through. I reckon Stroud sees that, though he didn't come out an' say so. No, back then, Nate, I was playing with a stacked deck. I found that out too late. What I didn't know, an' don't yet, is who was holding the other cards. Take it or leave it, that's the truth of it.'

Cooper straightened up from his leaning attitude. He said, 'Harve Beddoes meant what he said. That I can tell you. If there's shots fired he'll take in whoever's left standin'. If there is anybody. It won't matter a shit who sets it alight.'

Taber said, 'Old Harve, he gets me either way. If Josiah gets it done, nobody has to worry any more about John Taber except who'll pay the undertaker.' He smiled. 'They'd have to approach Stroud. If I take Josiah, Harve hauls me in. Bet he'll never have such a good day, the rest of his time in office. Well, right now, Nate, I'm heading down to the Ace Livery. Any notion where Gaul's at?'

'No. An' that's the truth, John.' He looked at the ground between his boots, then up at Taber. 'I could ask yuh to hand over that thing you're carryin', but all that'd do would be make damn' sure yuh didn't get an even break. Anyways, mebbe this man Rolt I hear about, he'd turn out to be a mite too quick for me.' He gave a slight shrug. 'I'm a deputy here. Yuh come out an' I give yuh due warnin'.'

'That you did, Deputy.'

Suddenly Cooper stuck out a hand. 'Luck.'

They shook on it. Taber nodded. He moved on. It was some distance to the Ace Livery. He had chosen not to go by way of the main street but by the back street on one of whose corners was the lumber yard. As a precaution, Taber thumbed the hammer-thong free and was walking steadily but unhurriedly.

On this street nothing seemed to be stirring, nothing disturbing the quiet there. A dog went sniffing along the line of a battered fence. Somewhere further along on the opposite side, there began the measured ringing of a black-smith's hammer. Taber could see blue smoke rising straight into the air from the forge. Somewhere else out of his view a horse whickered. Taber went pacing on.

It was possible that at some stage Gaul had been standing at some elevated window from which he would be able to see Taber come out of Maggie Corbin's. So he might well know that Taber was on the way. Forewarned is forearmed. Perhaps he had other eyes scanning the streets for him. Indeed, Taber considered that to be a probability. Every deck would turn out to be stacked in some way.

Some presentiment warned Taber that Gaul was in the vicinity. So far, however, he had not come into view. Taber took a quick glance back the way he had come. Back there in the distance, at the lumber yard corner, Deputy Cooper was watching. Cooper raised one hand slightly, then let it fall. He might just as well have called out that he intended staying there and that he would be watching Taber's back. Gratified, Taber acknowledged the deputy's signal, then turned and walked on. He was still in no hurry, his eyes shifting this way and that in a street where there were numerous premises used only for storage and which, therefore, offered plenty of places in which a man could stand, out of all sight.

It would indeed transpire that other eyes were following the progress of the tall, gaunt man along the middle of this back street. Taber's pace slowed even more and soon he came to a stop. Across to his right were some unkempt lots behind buildings whose frontages lay along the main street. Bunch grass and weeds and garbage abounded, the place alive with flies. Windows at the back of the buildings looked darkly blank but that did not necessarily mean much. He turned his head. To his left were other sun-warped structures, a couple of them abandoned stores, the window glass here shattered. There was a barn, its tall doors shut fast, and next to it a rough lot with rusting ironwork of unidentifiable origin buried among tangled weeds. Further along on that side was the hammer-ringing, smoky forge.

Taber walked on. He could not see the black-smith's yard in its entirety for there was a roof overhang covering some of it and a six foot, age-grey fence obscuring much of it when viewed from the street. He passed the forge. He had got some thirty feet beyond it when, for a reason he could not have explained, he looked back.

Still he could not see all of the interior of the forge, certainly not the anvil, where the steady hammering was still going on. What he now *could* see was the figure of a man, standing almost in shadow. A muscular man, he was stripped to the waist and wearing a leather apron. He had a dirty bandage wrapped around one of his hands. Hatless, the man was balding, a hedge of whitish hair on either side of his scalp.

Again Taber came to a halt. About seventy feet now separated Taber from the smith who, when Taber nodded, did not respond. The clanging sound of hammer on steel continued. Taber took a swift glance around him. Then, his attention returning to the smith in the yard, he began backing away until the distance increased to some eighty feet.

Then he called, 'Josiah!' There was no response. The clanging noises continued. Taber waited, then raised his voice. 'Josiah!' After only a matter of seconds the clanging ceased.

When Gaul came walking out from the forge, he nodded and said, 'John . . . '

Taber called, 'Another few strides an' you'd have got a clean shot. Thought better of you, Josiah.' That was not necessarily true. Gaul smiled.

Taber, in one way, wished he had been closer to the man so that he could see his eyes more clearly. To look for the ghost of an expression he believed that he had read while in the café. Though he was keeping his attention pinned on Gaul he was aware that the blacksmith had taken the opportunity to get himself as far as possible out of harm's way. If, as seemed inevitable, shooting started, the smith would have no wish to be behind one of the protagonists.

There was some slight movement, too, away down to the left and Taber could but hope that it might mean that Deputy Cooper would at least be a witness to whatever occurred. If Beddoes and Cobb were by now anywhere near, Taber had no way of knowing. But he did feel sure that there would be plenty of other observers, no doubt being very careful and discreet.

Now he came to the belief that he had read Josiah Gaul correctly, for seconds had now gone by, stretching to half a minute; then three-quarters. Unsure. Gaul must be unsure or by this time he would have made his move.

Taber was standing with his hands hanging loosely at his sides. Gaul, his left foot slightly advanced, had now put his right hand on the handle of his pistol. Unsure, so needing an edge, Taber thought. He took a few slow paces towards Gaul, then stopped. He reckoned the distance was about right, so he called, 'C'mon then, Josiah. Tell me, they paid you yet? Or does that come after? If you miss, an' you'll only get the one chance, they'll have saved their money.'

Gaul stood looking at him. Still the seconds went slipping by in utter silence and without a hint of movement. Taber's eyes were fastened on Gaul's eyes. Taber's attitude seemed almost negligent.

The slight dip of the left shoulder gave it away and it was enough of a signal to Taber. He drew smoothly. He had reckoned, all through, Gaul would try to get it done too fast. It was a fault seen often in those who were nervous. It made getting a first hit all that more uncertain.

And so it proved. Gaul's pistol banged, flaring and punching out smoke, but the lead went humming by. Taber was already walking in, and now, arm extended, he shot, the pistol bucking and smoking. Gaul bent forward abruptly as though bowing to an audience, his pistol swinging wide of his body. Taber stopped walking. Still bent half over, Josiah Gaul took a couple of shuffling sideways steps, then sat down hard, head hanging, his hat falling off, the pistol still gripped in his right hand but resting on the ground. The sudden outbreak of shooting had left behind it another uncanny silence. Taber stood with his whole attention on Gaul for maybe half a minute. Somewhere a horse whickered. Taber slid the Smith & Wesson down in the holster. Yet he did not turn his back on the man who had been shot.

Deputy Cooper came walking, his pistol drawn and pointing at Gaul. From somewhere behind Taber, Sheriff Beddoes and Deputy Cobb were coming at a run, their pistols also drawn and pointing at Taber. Cooper had arrived at the scene and was approaching the still-sitting figure of Josiah Gaul. Cooper bent forward and took the pistol away. When he straightened and looked towards Taber and nodded, Beddoes was saying, in some excitement, 'I give yuh fair warnin' mister. Cain't no ways say I didn't.'

Cobb was, of course, aggressive. 'I'll have that pistol.' He stepped up behind Taber and drew the Smith & Wesson from its holster.

At that moment the sitting Gaul tipped over and lay on his side in a near foetal attitude. Cooper left him, holstered his own weapon and, carrying Gaul's, a Remington, came over to where Taber and Cobb and Beddoes were. By this time numerous people had appeared and, at a little distance, stood watching proceedings.

Cooper said, 'It was Gaul drew on him.'

Loudly, Beddoes said, 'I don't give a good goddamn who drew on who an' when! This here feller was warned.

I give 'im clear warnin'. So he goes in the cage.'

There was to be no further discussion. Taber was led away. Cooper was assigned that task, maybe for having spoken up on Taber's behalf. The crowd that had gathered was growing. Now that the shooting was over, confidence had returned and Taber was called out to and even jeered, this, possibly, by those who had not actually witnessed all that had taken place.

When they arrived at the county jail, Taber took a chance and said, 'The way Harve is, I could be in here for a while. If he has his way he'll string out some damn' enquiry.' So he mentioned the soddies along Mavor Creek. 'That place is where I reckon the feller that stopped the stage went right after he shot at me. There's a trail but it's not easy to see. I went there, to the soddies, to ask some questions. I got nowhere. They were all set to put lead in me. They're real leery of Sam Stedman.

They think that if he took it into his head to clear 'em out, he'd do it. Maybe so. His boys could get it done inside an hour. But I'd put money on the notion that somebody out there knows something.'

Cooper thought about that and nodded. He swung the door to the cell open. As Taber walked inside, he said, 'I don't no ways agree with this, John, but I got no choice.'

'Understood,' Taber said. Cooper had not even bothered to get him to shuck his shellbelt.

Cooper left him. A short while later, however, Cobb and Beddoes returned to the county office. Beddoes came down and stood outside the cell.

'Gaul's sure dead. What yuh gonna do, mister, is cool off in here 'til I git my mind made up about yuh. Folks is all stirred up.' Taber thought he meant the merchants, in the main. 'Could be an inquiry. Could be we jes' decide to git shot o' yuh. There's a train through late afternoon, tomorrow. Fer points

119

north. There's a possibility yuh'll be on it.'

Taber did not say anything. He was left to himself. But later in the day they were back. There was no sign of Cooper. This time there was some noise. Beddoes and Cobb came into the county building herding three rowdy cowboys, probably hauled out of one of the saloons. While Beddoes kept an eye on them, Cobb said to Taber, 'Git your ass off'n that cot, mister.' Taber swung his legs down. He was taken out of the cell and led by Cobb to a smaller one further down the passage. Behind them Beddoes shoved the noisy cowboys into the one that Taber had been occupying. No sooner were they inside, however, than they began acting up worse.

Beddoes yelled, 'Aaron!' Cobb clanged Taber's cell door shut and, drawing his pistol, went to give some help to Beddoes. There seemed to be a lot of shoving and cursing but not much else to get excited about. Nonetheless,

Cobb got very red in the face and began shouting louder than the range men, which was no mean feat. So, by and by, the boys in the cell were settled down, and though still making tongue-noises, were locked in.

When Beddoes and Cobb had gone up to the office and shut the door behind them, Taber quietly took a look at the door to his own cell. Cobb had gone away and left the key in the lock.

* * *

Emily Voller was in the house behind the mercantile. Robert Voller was out in the yard checking over some boxes of merchandise lately arrived. The woman was deeply disturbed. She felt as though she was carring a lead weight inside her. Only a short while ago, Sheriff Beddoes had come by unexpectedly. Emily, at that time, had also been out in the yard, but it soon became clear that Beddoes did not want her to hear what he had to say. She had taken the unspoken hint and had gone indoors. But not very far indoors.

Beddoes and her husband had fallen into a deep conversation. Emily was quite sure that they had been talking about Taber. She had been able to hear only snatches of what had been said.

'. . . got the bastard in the cage . . . first step . . . leaving it to Cobb . . . feller gits out an' makes a run . . . by God it's gonna be his last . . . '

9

Night. Emily Voller had put on her cloak and was preparing to slip out while her husband was occupied elsewhere. It was not to be. Coming across to the house from the mercantile when he had not been expected, he demanded to know where she was going at this hour. This turned out to be the moment of confrontation that had been threatening to come for some while.

The older husband was sparked to immediate fury when she said, 'I know about Mr Beddoes and John Taber. I know that somehow they're going to give him the chance to get out of the jail and run. It's being done to give them the excuse to kill him. Who's behind this Robert? Really behind it? Not Beddoes. Not Cobb, even. What would they have to gain? No, they're the puppets. Somebody else has got hold of the strings. Is it you? Is it the merchants? Is it your great friend, Sam Stedman? If you don't know about it, why would Beddoes come here to tell you what's to happen?'

'You're forbidden to go out!' Voller shouted. 'I know damn' well yuh'd warn that bastard if yuh could! By God! My wife! I'll not have it! Yuh hear me?'

'Half of Charon must be able to hear you.'

'I don't give a damn! Men built this here town! The men that are here now, most of 'em. They'll say what goes here. I'll say what goes in this house. I won't have yuh takin' the part of the jailbird, Emily! I mean what I say!'

'Listen to you! One of the men! What you're doing is having other men do what you don't have the nerve to do for yourself! That man Gaul, for one. John Taber said he was second rate, that much I've heard. Where does that leave the creatures who hired him?'

'I'll not be defied in my own house this way! Take off that cloak an' make no move to go out of here tonight!'

'Whatever you say isn't going to make any difference. I'll not stand by and see any man shot down if I can do anything to prevent it. My mind's made up.'

She knew he was very angry indeed, but she did not expect what happened next, for such a thing had never happened before. In a blur of fury-driven movement, his open hand came arcing around and the solid slap against her cheek was as sharp as a small-calibre rifle shot. So hard was it that it knocked her sideways and she fell to her knees.

Elsewhere, Taber was out. It had been a whole lot easier than he had thought possible. The cowhands in the adjoining cell looked as though they were all asleep as, moving it only an inch at a time, he had eased open the cell door and stepped into the passageway. There had been no one in the front office. Lucky. Stepping as quietly as he could, he cast around for the Smith & Wesson that Cobb had taken from him but failed to find it. There were rifles and a shotgun in a glass-fronted cabinet, but it was locked and he did not have time to look for the key. And the cell key still haunted his mind. Getting this far had indeed been easy. Too easy was but the wraith of a further thought as he ventured outside the county building seeking shadows for concealment. He was moving step by careful step. The main street seemed very quiet.

They did not let him get far. From across on the opposite side a pistol banged. Stabbing flame. Lead came whanging into dry boards a mere half step behind Taber. Somebody with a higher opinion of his own shooting than was justified. Up ahead on the boardwalk outside a darkened building, his eyes caught quick movement. The black maw of an alley that he had now come to was enticing but because he now realized that he had been set up to be shot, escaping, he dare not go hastening into so obvious a trap. Instead, he took another option which likely would be unexpected. He turned very quickly and, his boots pounding on the boardwalk, ran back past the county office, then under orange lamplight outside a gunsmith's shop. Now he was taking a gamble that the men seeking to bring him down would hold off shooting towards the shop which was still open for business. Taber clawed the gunsmith's door open and ran inside.

The gunsmith, a bald man with eyeglasses and wearing a leather apron looked up in alarm as the man came bursting in. Then he gave a yelp of protest as Taber grabbed hold of an old .44 Remington that was lying on a bench, and ran on right through the shop to the back of the premises. Once there he ripped open the back door and went plunging out into a dark, weedy, refuse-littered yard. At least — if only for the moment — he was out of the trap.

At the far end of the yard there was a broken fence and at one corner of it he paused. Mainly through touch, he loaded the Remington, hoping that the weapon was in a usable condition, given where he had picked it up. Then, crouching down where he was, he could hear plainly the boots of men running. It would come as no surprise to him that there would be plenty of others besides Beddoes and his deputies out on the streets of Charon, all seeking him and no doubt with instructions to shoot on sight. A kind of fever overcame men when a hunt was on and that malaise would be running strongly now, of that he had no doubt.

Taber's guess was that S-Bar riders in town would have been roped in to join the hunt for him. If that was so, it would seem to confirm Stedman's hand in this. Taber had thought that if he remained unmoving in the darkness, eventually he might get the opportunity to slip away and reach a livery. They could have men watching those establishments, of course, and in that event he would have to try to get to one of the hitched horses on Main. For it was certain that one way or another he must find a horse and for a start get clear of the town. What he might do then he had no idea. Beddoes' actions had changed the whole game as far as Taber was concerned. Even the pistol in his hand was of limited use to him. If he were to be attacked by any man here who was not one of the regular lawmen, he would have no hesitation in defending himself. In that event he could scarcely be in any worse position than he was now. He doubted that any citizens or any S-Bar men would have been deputized. They would have been confident of nailing him as soon as he stepped out of the county building. But if one of the lawmen shot at him, he could not afford to shoot back. And they would know it.

Someone then did what Taber himself

had done, came right on through the gunsmith's shop. Taber, low down and squinting towards the man who was limned against the glow from within the gunsmith's, got the impression that it was one of Stedman's riders. Somewhere in front of where Taber was crouching, other men were passing along the back street. He hoped that by staying absolutely still he would not be noticed.

Then the man who had come out of the back door of the gunsmith's yelled, 'There's the bastard!' A pistol banged, flame flicking. Lead came slashing through a bunch of tall weeds very close to Taber. In his turn he blasted a shot that whanged into dry boards at the back of the shop. The man who had come out and fired went plunging back inside. Those who were on the back street began shouting and were coming towards Taber. In a desperate, crouching run he went towards where there was a small outbuilding and, in passing around the corner of it, fell over some object buried deep in the bunch-grass, causing a sharp pain in one of his shins.

Nearby there was another, much larger building all in darkness. Taber located a window with all the glass missing and went clambering in over the sill. He pitched full length into a room that was being used for the storage of crates and casks and he went blundering around among these, seeking the way to a door. There was one at the front that would take him out on to the main street but he did not want that. There was another at one side of the room, and this, albeit with some difficulty, he managed to draw open, gritty dust falling all over him.

Now he was in an alleyway. He moved along it away from the direction of the main street and into another back lot. Now, in this vicinity there was neither sight nor sound of the men searching for him. Taber pondered over his situation. The absence of sounds from the searchers was more concerning than being able to hear them, even had they been close at hand. Quietness might mean that they had gone elsewhere. It might also mean that they had simply gone to ground, that they were waiting for him somewhere along the back street or in any of the back lots. They would know that sooner or later he would have to make a move. All they would have to do was wait. Yet as they would be aware, he dare not double back and risk showing himself on the main street. Or could he? If he did, and managed to cross that street unseen or unrecognized, the hunters might well be thrown off, having sighted him across this side.

Taber slipped away and passed along the alley. At the far end, the main street end, he took a very cautious look. Pole lamps were still lit and there were lights in some of the establishments, but there was very little activity to be seen. It was probably that pistol shots had persuaded a good many people to get out of sight and seek safety until reassured that all was well again.

Taber came to the conclusion that boldness might well be the answer rather than trying to be circumspect and perhaps succeed only in drawing attention to himself. He pushed the Remington down in the holster and walked out from the cover of the alley across the wide street, looking neither left nor right. If he had made a bad mistake, then at any moment there might come a shout, a challenge to identify himself. Or worse, they could start shooting. Determinedly he walked on, still looking straight ahead. Lamplight from various buildings was pooled across the boardwalk. But there were numerous places of deep shadow too, and Taber, stepping on to the boardwalk, passed into one of these. He had got across. In the dark maw of an alley, he heard a man's voice, then a woman's. He realized that he must have just missed coming face to face with the man who had come out of a nearby door, on Main. As the man went by, Taber recognized Robert Voller.

Waiting until the man was far enough away, Taber came easing out of the deep shadows. Emily Voller was still standing there watching her husband's back as he departed along the boardwalk. Now there was a quick intake of breath as a man appeared, quite close to her. Then she saw who it was and said, in a low, urgent voice. 'John! Come inside, quickly!' She withdrew and he followed her inside the now dark doorway of the mercantile. She moved swiftly to close the door behind him. He could smell her perfume. 'Just follow me.' She led him through the jumbled mercantile, then out into the yard which separated mercantile and house. Lamps were glowing inside the house. In the yellowish spill from them he caught sight of her small face. It was impossible to overlook the swelling to her cheek.

Taber's voice was hard when he asked her, 'Did Voller do that to you?'

Softly she said, 'Yes.'

'Was it to do with me?'

'It's not important. It's done, that's all there is to it. It won't happen again.'

'But I've brought that on you . . . '

'I sought you out, John. You didn't come looking for me.'

'Nevertheless — '

She broke in, 'What you have to do is get away from here, and now. They'll scour the town for you. You can't afford to let it come daylight. There'd be nowhere to hide.'

'I was trying to get to one of the liveries, but I didn't make it.' Then, 'It wasn't 'til I was out of the county building that I realized they'd given me the chance to make a break. Cobb left a key in the cell door. They covered what they'd done by fetching in some half-drunk cowboys. I should've twigged it was all wrong. Keys are generally on a ring, all the keys together. I made a stupid move.'

'I found out about it. I tried to get out and warn you.'

'That was when he hit you?'

She nodded. 'But what's important now is you getting away. There's a horse in our barn, and a saddle. He's not the fastest horse in Charon but he's got plenty of stamina. He'll not let you down.'

'Emily, all that will bring you is a whole lot more trouble when he finds out. I can't let you take a risk like that. I'll have to find another mount somewhere.'

'John, the damage is already done. He'll not strike me again.' There was a new hardness in her tone. 'Come along. Quickly.' Taber could see that there was to be no dissuading her. He had the immediate sense that, as far as Emily Voller was concerned, a die had been cast, that she had already taken the first steps on a path from which there would be no turning back. Now, in the straw-smelling barn, she watched, pale-faced, as he lit a lantern. She asked, 'Where will you go?'

'South-west. To the soddies. I went there before but I got turned away real quick. I'll not be turned away again. Emily, I'm damn' sure that part of the answer I want is down there somewhere. Things that can be told, with a certain amount of persuasion. Things that'll help me. I'm not letting go, Emily. I'll not carry this brand they put on me for the rest of my days.' Then, 'What about you?'

'You can rely on me, John. I'll look for a way to help.'

'Emily, you'll need to take great care.'

'I'll take care.' Then, in a very quiet voice, 'They brought that Josiah Gaul here to kill you. That became all too plain. I saw nothing, but there are one or two people ready to admit that he left you no option.'

'They're outnumbered by those that

see it the other way or just want to stand back an' say nothing.' He looked at her directly. 'Your Robert, was he a part of that?'

Wearily she shook her head. 'Truly, I don't know. So I can't say that.'

'But it's possible?'

'Among some of the other traders, maybe. Yes. Men you hardly ever hear of.'

'I thought that.'

'And there's Beddoes and Cobb and Sam Stedman. They've got to have been involved in some way. Maybe not directly. Maybe just turning a blind eye. But now that the man's dead and they've got you on the run, I doubt if all of it will ever come out. Tracks will be well covered.'

'They'd be wrong to think I'll just give up because of this.'

'Stedman, he'll want you gone. And he's got men who won't question orders.'

'Sam's wanted that since I first showed my face.'

'Yes, but there's more to it now. It's more urgent.'

'How?'

'In just a few days' time, a couple of congressmen are due to come here.'

'Congressmen? Why? Who are they?'

'I didn't hear their names. What I do know is that they're coming to talk with Sam Stedman. The kind of men who are important to him. Important in what he wants to do. Sam will want to be seen as the strong man. The man who's in control. But a man with clean hands. So, eventually, more power, greater wealth.'

'Well, you're right. He sure won't want me here, still in his way an' causing a ruckus,' Taber said. 'He'll want me 'way out of the county. One way or another.' The horse, a bay, saddled, he led it out of the barn. Emily put out the lantern. 'I'll never be able to repay you for this, Emily. But take no more risks on my account.' Briefly, she came close to him. Again he caught the smell of her perfume. She stretched up on her toes, hands laid against his chest, and her lips brushed his cheek.

Taber swung up into the saddle. He looked at her one more time, the pale wash of her small face in the dark, then walked the horse out of the yard and made his way, still unhurriedly, out on to a back street. Nearing the limits of the town, he did not see the man until only a couple of yards from him, a quirly glowed. He passed by so close that even in the night's gloom, the other must surely have recognized Taber, the man being hunted. No word passed between them. Taber's horse walked on, the rider's back now turned to the smoker in the darkness. Taber headed steadily away from Charon. Behind him, Deputy Nate Coper had become engulfed by the night.

Fifty yards beyond the town, however, he was noticed by someone else, an S-Bar hand, perhaps posted to keep a watch along the trail southward. When he was challenged, Taber gave no answer. The lone man did nothing for a short time, clearly caught in two minds. Then he fired off a pistol. Once . . . twice. That, no doubt, was an agreed signal to fetch others. Now Taber put spurs to the solid bay. If it did not, as Emily had told him, have great speed, he must now get the jump on the pursuers who would soon come riding out of Charon. He had to put distance between himself and them while they were still getting ready to ride.

Emily Voller was at the Ace Corral and Livery, arguing with the liveryman about the advisability of a woman, alone, setting out (to some destination unspecified) at such an hour. And anyway, everybody knew that there was a desperate man being hunted. The old man gave up when she became sharply spoken and demanded that he get ready the buggy and pair that she needed. Ten minutes later, shaking his head, he watched her, buggy whip in hand, swathed in a hooded cloak, heading off into the darkness.

They were out after Taber right enough, about ten riders, but he had no idea who they were. Cobb, perhaps. Beddoes. Some of the townsmen. Almost certainly some of the riders from the S-Bar. And they had done well. Although Taber had got what he considered was a good start on them, they were coming fast and were chasing him with great purpose and with what seemed to be an almost uncanny perception of his line of ride. Nonetheless, he led them a dance. And he had taken care to move more or less at right angles to the direction which, if he could shake these bastards off, he intended going.

Now he had stopped and was down out of the saddle, standing at the horse's head. He was in an area of high brush, and the sounds of the chasing riders who, having passed by the place where he was, and at a distance of only some forty yards, were becoming less distinct as they rode on.

Still, he waited no more than two or three minutes until he felt quite sure that they had not stopped or doubled back before he remounted and set the horse to a gentle, loping stride, allowing it to recover from the rigours of the recent chase. He had no notion of how long the posse might continue on, pursuing nothing, but he had to assume that it would not continue for long. Soon he would have to push the bay harder.

Shortly before sun-up, in the grey hour, the bay picketed among the leafy trees along the twisting creek, Taber drew the Remington and prepared to await his chance, fervently hoping that he would be able to get right in, this time, without being under the threat of a rifle and shotgun.

Presently, a stoop-shouldered man coming back from the creek, having gone there to fill a wooden pail, heard the ratchety click of a hammer being cocked, and stopped dead.

'Easy, mister,' Taber said softly.

'Now you tell me who your head man is. The man whose word always goes. There's got to be one.' These were the soddies along Mavor Creek, blue smoke beginning to rise from some of them.

In a husky voice the man said, 'Bart Edmond.'

'Where?'

'The one up yonderways.'

'Go in close to it. Call him. Friendly. If you don't do it right it's your backbone the lead's gonna punch through.' The water-carrier must have known from the low but hard voice that he was not hearing an idle threat.

Nearer to the soddy that he had pointed out, he called, 'Bart? Need some help here . . .'

Blinking in the early light, Bart Edmond emerged. Then he saw the man holding the pistol. Taber recognized Edmond as the man who, on his earlier visit here, had put a rifle on him.

Taber said, 'This time I'll take no shit, mister. Four years back there was a bastard rode in here. Hid out here. Now I want answers about that man.' Something in Edmond's eyes, an uncertainty, fear even, told Taber that there was something more here beyond what might have gone on four years ago. Neither Edmond nor the water-carrier, though no doubt they were desperate to do so, could call a warning to the man who now appeared, unsuspecting, from another of the soddies. Taber said, 'Just keep coming, Dave. Slow and easy.'

Dave Radich, however, stopped in his tracks. He did not approach until Taber extended the pistol-arm and squinted along the barrel. Dave then resumed his approach. But very slowly. He was not armed. Behind him, wearing only a light shift, the girl, Nell Rorke, stood in the soddy's doorway. Taber did not mince matters. In his mind it was all coming together. When Radich was three feet from him, Taber said, 'Far enough, Dave.' Radich, swallowing hard, sweating, his eyes, which were still puffed from sleep, wide open, had no voice. Taber knew that this, of all times, was the one to push this business. 'Come here a lot, Dave? That so? Today. Yesterday. Four years back?' Then his face a mask of anger, 'You let me take the fall, Dave.' Before Radich could say anything, the barrel of the Remington was whipped across in an arc, cracking against Radich's right cheekbone. Radich went down like a shot dog. When, involuntarily, Edmond took a step, Taber said, 'Take one more an' I'll blow your belly button through your asshole.' Edmond stopped. Dave Radich, a bloodied welt across his face, was trying to get to his feet. 'Now you an' me, Dave, we'll take us a trip into Charon. You've got a tale to tell.'

10

Not far out of Charon, so far not having sighted other riders, Taber, riding behind Dave Radich, told him to leave the trail and to pass among some cottonwoods. This was an area that Taber had observed before when noting places in which he might take cover if that became necessary. In a bunch-grass clearing among those trees were the remnants of buildings. They were all that now remained of some long-gone sodbuster's home. The chief structure had all but crumbled away, though a couple of the walls were still standing. Three outbuildings were no more than heaps of greying lumber.

Taber needed some time to work out what moves he should make once he got as far as Charon. How he could manage to get said what he needed to say before some mad bastard up and shot him. He told Radich to get down. Radich did. No arrogance now. No posturing. But he had stubbornly refused to admit anything.

Not able to talk quite clearly because of his swollen face, he had still insisted, 'Yuh can't prove nothin'.'

'We'll see.'

They picketed the horses among the nearest of the trees. Radich was hang-headed, paying much attention to the right side of his face, so swollen that the eye was almost closed.

Taber paused, listening. He had believed that they had got into this place, which was in fact about a mile short of Trubshawe's horse ranch, without having been seen. But there could be no doubt that a bunch of horsemen were close at hand. Taber nodded towards the ruins of the homestead and he gave Radich a heavy shove.

'Get in there and lie down.' Taber followed Radich in and got down on one knee, drawing the Remington.

Hardly had he done so than the sounds of the horses ceased.

Almost at once, however, a voice that Taber recognized as Sam Stedman's, called, 'Taber! I'm givin' yuh one minute to git your ass out of there!'

Taber called in return, 'Save your breath, Sam. You want me, send your boys in. If six come in, three won't come out . . . Up to you.'

They must have moved in close, for Taber could hear a muttering of talk. An argument, maybe. Presently Stedman's voice came again.

'That Dave Radich yuh got in there?'

'It is. Is Beddoes with you? Is Cobb?'

A short pause. Stedman called, 'Nope. Neither.'

'That's a pity, Sam. Doesn't give you any authority. You'd best tread real careful.' He waited for that to sink in. Stedman was no fool. 'What I'm about to do is take Radich into Charon. We're gonna have us a talk with Harve Beddoes. If you want to put yourself above the law, Sam, that's your decision. It might not go down well in certain places. Anyway, in a couple of minutes I'm coming out of here an' I'll have Dave Radich along with me.' He waited for that to sink in. 'Make one move, you or any of your boys, an' Radich will never see sundown. You want to find out if I'm bluffing, then have some idiot push it.' Taber knew that it was a bold and uncertain card to play, but he was holding no other. He could not afford to be pinned down here, trying to figure out what they were up to while trying to watch Dave Radich as well. What he was banking on was that Stedman, the man of power but the political-man-to-be, so he thought, would hardly be likely to impress the expected congressmen after a shooting. Nonetheless, Taber was kept hanging, for a silence fell. He began to wonder if all the talk from Stedman had been a ploy to cover the careful approach of others, to catch Taber off guard. Several minutes went by.

Then Stedman called, 'There'll be no shootin'. We'll hold back.'

Taber motioned for Dave Radich to stand up. He told him to walk across to where the horses were. Pistol in hand, Taber followed. They mounted up.

When they came walking their horses out from the shelter of the cottonwoods, the first thing they saw was the group of horsemen, all still mounted, Sam Stedman fronting them, all S-Bar riders. No pistols were drawn. Taber's was pointed at Dave Radich. How far Stedman would hold back was yet to be seen. Some fifty yards on, Taber took a quick look back to see that the S-Bar party was just beginning to move. Among them he could see Augie Leech and Matt Jenner — Jenner, with a score to settle and probably ravening to get it done.

They went bobbing on. Another mile, going steadily, the distance between the pair and the group of riders still some fifty yards. They were now passing Arn Trubshawe's horse ranch. Trubshawe was standing near his barn. His mouth had fallen open watching this sombre cavalcade go by. Taber did not even glance Trubshawe's way. He had no wish to involve the old man and, for all he knew, open him up to some kind of retribution. So Trubshawe's buildings and corrals gradually fell behind them and presently the sharp angles of the Charon roofs were lifting ahead of them. Taber realized that the real test was now to come.

At the top end of the main street, Taber saw what he did not wish to see. Harve Beddoes and Aaron Cobb came walking out of the county office. A short distance away, there, too, was Deputy Cooper, thumbs hooked in his belt, watching.

Beddoes called, 'Hold up, there!' There would be no doubt that he had seen the pistol in Taber's hand and could see also the sorry state of Dave Radich. Cobb was looking at Taber fixedly and it was far from certain that the deputy would not take it in his head to draw his own pistol. But Beddoes had made no move, so in the end Cobb must have thought it best to wait.

Behind Taber, now, there came the sounds of Sam Stedman and his riders closing the gap. They came to a halt only a few yards behind.

Stedman, perhaps also thinking that Beddoes, or more likely Cobb, might draw pistols in an attempt to make an arrest, called out, 'If any man draws, Taber'll blow Dave's lamp out. He's said that an' I reckon he means it.' There was something different about Stedman. It was in his tone of voice. It was as though he was not quite sure of himself.

Cobb was now showing renewed signs of impatience. He had put his hand on the pistol. It was Cooper's voice that was heard next.

'It'd be a fool move, Aaron.'

Cobb's round face turned to look at the other deputy. Beddoes muttered something to Cobb. Cobb's hand fell away from the pistol. His face had coloured, though, and there was a sense of words yet to be exchanged between him and Cooper. Taber knew they were all balancing on a taut wire and that the smallest thing might tip them over into a shoot. He was well aware of Matt Jenner, in particular at his back, without Cobb losing control. Beddoes was clearly frustrated, standing there blinking at Taber.

To Dave Radich, but loudly enough for it to be heard all around, he said, 'Walk him on.' Then, in a much lower tone, 'Past that next street on the left, angle left. That store there's empty. When we get there, get down. That's where we're going.'

Radich gave him a look, but said nothing and walked the horse on. When they reached the empty store they hitched the horses to the tie-rail and crossed the boardwalk. The door was unlocked. Taber nudged Radich aside but, holding the Remington to the man's mouth, called to Beddoes,

'Now listen to this, Harve. We're gonna wait right in here 'til you get done what I want. I want Jane Reed brought in from the S-Bar. You an' me are gonna ask that lady a few questions.' Then he said, 'The man that robbed the stage, he hid out at the soddies on Mavor Creek.' Taber moved his head slightly. 'Just like this feller was doing. If I could've handled 'em all I'd have brought in the whole goddamn' bunch of 'em. This *hombre*'s woman for sure.' When Beddoes did not respond, 'Radich, here, he stays with me 'til you've got Jane Reed an' we've had our talk.' To Stedman, he said, 'I'd advise you to keep a hard rein on the clowns behind you. I'll not stand for any smart moves from any of 'em.'

Beddoes and Cobb had moved closer. The S-Bar had walked their horses in and now formed a semi-circle on Main, the horses shifting, tossing heads, and there was the occasional clink of a bit-chain. Hard faces were staring at

Taber and the man he had under his pistol.

Sam Stedman was leaning down in his saddle muttering something urgently to Beddoes. Stedman had not reacted when his sister's name had been mentioned by Taber, but that did not mean that he would not have something to say about the matter. Matt Jenner, his pocked face shining, had his small eyes fixed on Taber, boring into him it seemed. Taber now thought that if anybody snapped and set it all alight it was even more likely to be Jenner than Cobb.

Stedman straightened in his saddle. Now he turned his head, looking at his riders.

'Sheriff Beddoes an' me are of a mind. The man that's got to be looked out for is Dave Radich. For the minute, Taber holds the high cards. We cain't go in bull-headed.'

At this, Taber backed Radich inside the empty store and shut the door. Out of a grimy window he could see that nobody had moved, but there was talk going on between the lawmen and Stedman and among the S-Bar hands. They had done a lot of riding in the past few hours and nothing to show for it. And now Taber was only a matter of yards from where they sat their horses.

A few townsmen had gathered. Some were beginning to call out for Beddoes to take a hand.

'Sheriff, yuh gonna let that mouthy jailbird call the tune?'

Some of these men had come out of a nearby saloon, and Stedman, reverting now to his familiar style, and before Beddoes himself could respond, bellowed back at them. 'Mr Beddoes is in charge here! He don't need whiskey advice! He'll do what's best. John Taber's got a man held in that place who's done nothin' to deserve gittin' shot down. It cain't be rushed. I'm here, along with these riders o' mine to make damn' sure Mr Beddoes gits help if he says he needs it. Best thing for yuh to do is git the hell off this street. We got a duty to see the law's upheld.' This was Stedman the politician talking. And though by no means convinced, for feeling had been running against Taber, and mounting, day by day, the townsmen slowly dispersed.

In the doorway of the mercantile stood Robert Voller. For the sake of appearances he nodded his approval to Sam Stedman, but it was a worried, dour Voller who then withdrew inside his premises. Last night his wife had gone, and he had not the slightest idea where. As the hours had dragged by, Voller, sleepless, endlessly drinking coffee, had been torn between keeping the matter to himself and summoning one of the deputies to report her missing. Though there had not been such a case for several years, women had been known to come to harm in and around Charon. In the past, it had usually turned out to be the result of some alley-drunk grabbing hold and going too far. Unsavoury, but not unknown. Voller had, therefore, scoured the night streets, the yards and back-lots and alleys himself, but all to no avail. Emily had vanished. No note. Nothing. Bitterly, he now recalled the anger that there had been between them in recent hours and days. So now he was ravaged by worry and guilt. It had been a grave mistake to lose his temper and strike her.

But through the big window of the mercantile he stared malevolently across the street at the place where he knew Taber to be. That man was at the very heart of Voller's troubles, for it had been he who had been the cause of that violent dispute between man and wife. Like others, today, in Charon, for the life of him he could not understand why both Beddoes, who after all was the county law and Stedman, the man of great influence, had not taken a much stronger line with this man Taber. For both of those men, it seemed out of character. And now the entire group, lawmen and S-Bar, had moved away from the front of the empty store, out of Voller's view. Surely the whole matter was not to be allowed to die because one hostage, and a drunken loudmouth at that, had been put at pistol-point by a man who was a known felon.

Stedman, however, was by no means as inactive or as impotent as Voller imagined. Further along the main street, taking Beddoes aside, he said, 'Let's wait it out, Harve. At least wait 'til sundown. Now, how about goin' back down there an' callin' out to Taber, tell him yuh've already sent for Mrs Reed? That way we'll buy some time to git somethin' worked out here. I'll tell yuh now, Harve, I'll not be beat by this jailbird. An' there's no chance that I'll see Mrs Reed humiliated by him. I've told her already that she's got to stay away from the town while he's still here. He's got some goddamn' bee in his bonnet about her, an' by God I'll not tolerate it!'

Beddoes nodded. It made sense to

buy some time. Cool matters down in some quarters. Stedman now told his riders to back off. Quietly he drew to one side Leech and Jenner.

'When I'm ready, yuh'll be told when to move an' what to do.' Some bills changed hands. 'Go git them boys a drink, but by God, have 'em take it easy. I don't want no mistakes made when the time comes.'

Going away, Leech and Jenner exchanged looks. You had to hand it to the man. He was nobody's fool. Before long, this Taber bastard would find that out to his cost.

Plenty of others were interested to know what was going to happen over this strange stand-off, when would it be resolved and if it might possibly be done without bloodshed. The odd little banker, Stroud, for one. He had been an intrigued, though unobtrusive spectator of the recent events. The white-whiskered Arn Trubshawe was another. Mystified by his witnessing the passing by of John Taber and

Dave Radich and the steady, implacable tracking of those two by no less than Sam Stedman and a bunch of his S-Bar riders, the horse rancher had quietly followed them all in. Whatever had taken place in the past, whatever dire accusations had been made and what was said to be evidence produced in the court, old Trubshawe reckoned that he was at least as good a judge of men as he was of horses. John Taber had never struck him as being anything other than a forthright and honest man. A man with a rough past, maybe, but in these Western lands, that certainly did not set him apart.

In all of the comings and goings after Taber had taken his hostage out of sight, Sheriff Beddoes had failed to notice that his second deputy, Nate Cooper, seemed to have dropped out of sight. Beddoes resolved to give the man a flea in his ear as soon as he reappeared.

In the abandoned store, Dave Radich, sore and subdued, had nonetheless begun complaining that his damaged face needed treatment. In no mood to listen to him, Taber told him to shut up.

'One of these days, Dave, you'll get your turn in the cage. When you do, one of the things you're gonna learn is what it is to get hurt. There are always too many for one man to handle. Then, when you go down, the boots go in. If you whine about it, they do it over again. An' again, 'til you stop whining.' Taber was standing to one side of a dirty window, doing his best to see the whereabouts of Beddoes and Cobb. Or Stedman. Since Beddoes had yelled out that Mrs Reed had been sent for, they had all disappeared. Taber thought he could see the ample-bodied Aaron Cobb across the other side of the street, standing just inside the entrance to an alley. But Beddoes was nowhere to be seen. Nor was Sam Stedman or any of the riders who had been with him. But Taber was harbouring no illusion that the rancher and his men would have gone away. Someone had taken the horses from the tie-rail out front.

Taber, telling Radich to get down on the floor and stay there, went prowling among the empty crates and casks which had been left in this dusty place. He examined a side-door. It was locked. And just beyond what turned out to be a thin partition he found a narrow flight of steps leading to upper rooms. Taber came back and told Radich to get back on his feet. When he did, still complaining, Taber led him to the flight of steps and followed him up to a room above, this too, at the front of the building.

Up here there were more crates and some bulky burlap sacks. Filthy windows overlooked the main street. Taber went over the room carefully and made up his mind what he would do if he had to. But that was for a later time.

To Radich he said, 'Sit on the floor, up against the wall on that side. Don't go near the windows.'

Radich, still mumbling his complaints, did so. Taber, too, settled down to wait. He could only hope that Beddoes' assurance that Jane Reed would be brought in to the town just as he had demanded, was the truth For a moment or two, Taber closed his eyes. When he opened them he saw that Radich was staring at him.

'Don't take a chance on it, Dave. You'd never make it.'

Radich scowled at him. Then, clearly both curious and unsettled, asked, 'This here Reed woman. What yuh want with her?'

'Thought you'd know that, Dave.'

'What?'

'She was *there*, Dave. That day at the stage.'

Radich's eyes were foxy. 'That there feller was masked. Everybody knows that.'

'She can still tell me things, mask or no mask.'

'Tell yuh what? What's there to tell?

They all give evidence. Yuh come up stinkin' of it.'

'Dave, I *know* who it was. There's others that know, as well. An' there's others again, who'll have guessed.'

'This is all shit.'

'Shit, Dave, is four years locked away among scum for something somebody else did. That's what shit is, Dave.'

Radich withdrew into a surly silence. But his mind was restless. Back at the soddies, Taber had outright accused him. Now there was all this business over the Reed woman.

When the day was well advanced, a buggy drawn by a pair of horses was travelling a trail from the S-Bar ranch towards Charon. Driving it was Emily Voller. Alongside her sat Jane Reed. The confrontation was behind them. The denials, the tears, the virtual admission of doubt behind them, too. Now the passenger had withdrawn into herself as the miles rolled under the wheels of the buggy. Normally a strong-willed woman, Jane

Reed would have to admit that, over this matter she had been no match for the smaller but very determined Emily Voller whom she was already acquainted with and who, in spite of clearly having been injured, had kept at Jane Reed until the other woman's resolve had crumbled.

'*You were never sure about it, were you? About it being John Taber?* (This, after a prolonged attack.) No answer. '*Were you? Answer me, Jane! Believe me, I'm in no humour to be lied to! Neither is John. Not any more.*' No answer. But a small shake of the head. And then another. Stronger.

The buggy went rolling on.

Towards sundown, in Charon, Beddoes, coming together with Cobb and Sam Stedman, said, 'We got to do somethin' soon. We cain't let this bastard go on holdin' all the cards.'

'There's another man's life bein' risked,' Stedman said. 'But I know it's got to be done, an' soon. He'll be lookin' fer Mrs Reed to git here an' start askin' questions soon.' Then, 'There's other things I got to do. I need Matt Jenner an' Augie Leech. Do nothin' 'til I git back.' They watched his big figure departing. Cobb smiled. Time and luck was running out fast for John Taber. Jailbird.

11

Night had almost come down. There was a heavy greyness abroad. Everything outside had lost its sharpness. No one had lately approached the place where Taber was holed up with his hostage.

That did not mean that nothing had been happening. With Nate Cooper still nowhere to be found, Aaron Cobb had got ready a dozen lanterns. Six of these had been lined up in front of the boardwalk out in front of the place where Taber was. The other six had been set out in the rough yard behind that place. All had now been lit. Beddoes had toured around various establishments, including the mercantile, advising people to keep their lamps lowered, if lamps had to be lit at all, for the duration of the night. Thus the front and the back of the old store would be illuminated and stand out strikingly in the otherwise near-darkened town.

Sam Stedman had not been idle, either. His men were no longer in the saloons. Matt Jenner, who, of all of them, badly wanted to be involved when the chance at Taber came, had been sent up on to the roof of a building next door to the mercantile. He was to lie there, rifle in hand, watching the place across the street. But Stedman had placed a firm stricture on the surly rider, one that could not have been misunderstood.

'A clear shot at Taber is one thing. But anything happens to the man he's took in there an' I'll personally peg your hide out in the brush.' And that had not been all of it. Stedman had despatched Augie Leech out to the S-Bar. 'Take this message to Mrs Reed. What she has to do is stay right out there on the ranch. This man Taber is real dangerous. He's sure dangerous to *her*. It's important she understands that. Don't take no from her. That's my instruction. Now git gone.'

Not long after, nearing Charon, the two women aboard the buggy thought that they could see some movement ahead of them. Indeed, it turned out to be a single rider who, long before they got to him, veered away from their line of approach and went riding by some yards to their left. If Jane Reed had recognized the rider in the brief moments of passing, as Augie Leech, she did not mention that fact to Emily. For some while she had not said anything at all.

In Charon, in the upper front room of the derelict store, Taber was having some problems with Dave Radich. Not only had Radich been continuing his complaints about the pain in the side of his face, now grossly swollen, but he had been threatening to call out to anyone below who might be listening. To call out to let them know exactly where Taber was. Taber told him to shut up.

'What yuh gonna do? Yuh gonna blow my head off?'

Taber said, 'You work it out for yourself, boy. Get 'em to make a rush. See if I do it. *They* reckon I'd do it. If they didn't think so, I'd never have got you as far as the door of this dump.'

Radich thought it over. Maybe he found some sort of logic in it. Anyway, it quietened him for a time. Then he said, 'They won't no ways git that Reed woman to come here. She wouldn't want to. Even if she did, Sam Stedman wouldn't let her come.'

'We'll wait. We'll see.'

Again Radich came back to what had been nagging at him earlier. 'What yuh want her for, anyways?'

'I said it before. She was on that stage.'

'There was others on it.' It was like a fly buzzing around Radich's head, irritating him.

'Long gone. The driver. The messenger. An old man. Likely he's dead by this. An' some other feller.

172

The one that took a shot at the man who'd done the holdup.'

'An' hit yuh,' Radich said, even sniggering.

'He missed him. The man running from the stage was the one that shot at me an' hit me,' Taber said.

'The law didn't reckon so. That jury, they didn't reckon so. Miz Reed, whatever she says, ain't no ways gonna change that.'

Taber did not argue with him further. Instead, he went across and squatted down alongside Radich, who was still sitting against a wall. Taber removed Radich's red bandanna. Taber folded it and tied a knot in the middle of it. He then shoved the knot inside Radich's mouth and knotted the bandanna tightly at the back of the man's neck. Radich was making protesting noises, grunting and moving his head this way and that. The tightness of the gag was maybe causing more pain to his ravaged face.

Taber took a careful look from one

of the windows. The pane was so grimy that he could see nothing distinctly, only a pool of light coming from lanterns that had been set out on the street, not far from the boardwalk. Almost everything else seemed to have been darkened. If he tried to walk out of this place he would do so as a well-lit target. Taber thought about his next move.

Out on the trail the buggy was still moving along. Emily, long reins to the loping pair in hand, buggy whip in the other, was reluctant to push the horses too hard in this gathering dark, trusting to the horses to stay on the trail. Then her senses picked up some change. She glanced over her shoulder. Then Jane Reed spoke for the first time in a long while.

'He's coming. Following us.' The horseman who had gone by only a minute or so ago.

Emily shook the reins and clicked her tongue to increase the pace of the pair. It had been done instinctively, for there was no way that the buggy would be able to outrun this rider, whatever his purpose might turn out to be. It had been no more than a gesture from a woman who was travelling a dark trail, unarmed, and who was being reminded that this was still a raw and sometimes unruly land. The horseman, as could be expected, was gathering the buggy in. And so quickly that Emily surrendered to the inevitable, hauling back on the reins, slowing the horses and finally bringing the vehicle to a stop.

The horseman arrived, drawing rein, his mount crabbing sideways then in a semi-circle, tossing its head, blowing. Positive recognition now caused Jane Reed to speak up.

'Mr Leech? This is Mrs Reed. What is it you want?'

'Miz Reed,' Leech said. 'Got sent out with a message fer yuh. From Mr Stedman hisself. He's in town right now.'

'Well, you've had a ride for nothing,

Mr Leech. But you can tell me what his message is and then ride on ahead of us. Tell my brother that I'm on my way in. I can talk with him then.'

'Ma'am, that's jes' the problem. Mr Stedman, he said to tell yuh that on no account was yuh to go into Charon. Not yet awhile. That feller Taber, he's got a pistol on Dave Radich an' he's holed up in a dump on Main. They're fixin' to git him out o' there 'thout Dave gittin' shot.'

Emily said, 'I know about John Taber. He'll not willingly shoot anybody. John Taber's the reason we — the reason that Mrs Reed is heading into Charon at this hour. So we'll need to get on our way, Mr Leech. But we'd be glad of your protection the rest of the way.'

Leech's horse was still on the move, stepping, shaking its head, its rider limned against the lighter darkness of the sky.

'Miz Reed, the boss, he was sure set on yuh stayin' away from town.

Said I had to make sure yuh got that message.'

Emily knew that if Leech was allowed to go on arguing there was just a chance that Jane Reed might lose her nerve. For John Taber's sake, especially in his present predicament, it was imperative that such a thing did not come to pass.

She said, 'Today I've been all the way to the S-Bar and now I'm almost back in Charon. There's no chance that I'm going to turn back now. Not for Mr Stedman or anybody.' She had spoken firmly in the hope that the man would quit arguing and back off. It was not to be. And Emily began to realize how determined Leech was to stop their going any further.

'Cain't 'low it, ma'am. Not no way. I got my orders from Mr Stedman hisself.' The voice had roughened somewhat. Leech did not fancy being thwarted and certainly not by some woman.

Emily, however, decided to test it to

the limit. She clicked her tongue and shook the reins. The pair walked on.

For a moment or two Leech was taken unawares, then he hauled his mount around and set it bounding after the rolling buggy. Leech rode to the head of the near-side horse, reached down and seized the bridle, tugging at it until the wagon pair, unsettled, slowed to a walk and then stopped. All pretence of politeness in the presence of Stedman's sister was now abandoned. Leech now reached down and grabbed hold of the reins and pulled them sharply out of Emily's grasp.

'Yuh ain't been listenin' to me. This here rig's gotta be turned 'round an' took back to S-Bar.'

Emily was deeply angry. It was as though she had been physically manhandled by this stinking Stedman hard-nose. And the pain and humiliation of having been struck by her own husband was still fresh in her mind.

'Mr Leech, you're making a very big

mistake. Give me back the reins and get on your way. You can please yourself whether that's to Charon or the S-Bar. Neither you nor Sam Stedman will tell me where I'm to go or when.'

'Git down off'n the buggy,' Leech said.

'Never!'

In the gloom, Emily was appalled to see that Leech's right hand was now resting on the handle of his pistol. She heard Jane Reed gasp and say, 'Mr Leech!'

Even as Jane Reed spoke, Leech made as though to draw the pistol. Perhaps it was a move to convince Emily Voller that she must do as he had told her. It was then that Emily, still gripping the buggy-whip, brought it slicing down across the right arm of the mounted man, fetching a yell from him and a toss of the head from the horse. Without hesitating, Emily struck again with the whip, this time angling it sideways. It caught Leech full across the face and he screamed in pain, and with both of his gloved hands, grabbed at one of his eyes. The horse went backing off, its rider now swaying in the saddle.

Briefly, Emily got down and retrieved the now trailing reins, scarcely hearing Jane's gasp of, 'Oh, Emily!' As quickly as she could, Emily got back up on the seat and shook the reins and started the buggy moving. Augie Leech was still making noises, but horse and rider were now behind the two women, swallowed up in the night. And now Emily laid the whip to the pair, setting them to a faster pace, trusting to luck that one of the buggy wheels would not strike a stone or find a hole large enough to cause damage, or worse, hurl them both from the seat. Emily kept the horses at it until, up ahead of them, they could see against a faint glow, the rise of the Charon roofs.

On the main street of the town, out in front of the store where Taber had taken Dave Radich, the six lanterns were still glowing. Off in the darkness,

Stedman said to Beddoes, 'Some time, they got to git some shuteye. We'll leave it a while longer, then we'll move. Front an' back at the same time. Matt's still up on that roof. There's no way Taber, if he's a mind to try, is gonna git out.'

Taber, and the tightly gagged Radich, were no longer in the upper room. Taber had got up on a couple of stacked-up crates and forced open a skylight, and both were now lying on the roof. There was a parapet at the front some two feet high, and it was behind this that Taber had told Radich to lie.

Taber's object in coming up here was to try to get a clear look at the street and maybe pin-point where the men had been placed; then do the same at the back. The next-door building was across an alley some four feet in width, and he thought that, if it came to it, it might just be necessary to jump across to the next roof, to descend some distance from this place. He was covering options. For as time had gone by he had come to the conclusion that Stedman would do all that he could to keep Jane Reed away from Charon — no matter what Beddoes had promised. As far as Stedman and Beddoes were concerned, Taber was a man on the run, and a dangerous one at that. Remember Josiah Gaul. So he must be dealt with accordingly.

Cautiously, Taber took a look over the parapet. The glow from the lanterns that had been set out reached well beyond the middle of the street. Beyond that were grey shadows, then a deeper darkness, for all of the buildings across there had had their lamps turned out.

The lighter dark of the moonless sky silhouetted the roofs and parapets. Directly opposite, next door to Voller's mercantile, was a narrow building which now engaged Taber's attention. Just for a moment he believed that his eye had caught a flicker of movement. On the roof. Taber sank down behind the parapet. If they had, say, a rifleman there, then both he and Radich could be in very serious trouble.

12

Phena Radich had been in Stedman's ear, but what she had been saying to him, others had not been able to hear, for Stedman had drawn her away out of earshot. Now they were standing together under an awning outside the Western Bank and Loan, which was 'way along the main street. Cobb was observing them. A handsome woman, Phena Radich, and given any encouragement, Cobb would have sought to get to know her better. He had received none. Cobb studied Stedman. For all his well-earned reputation for always being in control, no matter what was happening, Stedman was looking somewhat uncomfortable and was being very attentive to what the woman was saying. Cobb had always had his theories about them. He believed that Beddoes knew something, but Beddoes was a man who watched his own ass when it came to dealing with the likes of Stedman. He had always kept a close mouth, there. If indeed there was anything to know. Yet not only was Phena Radich talking with the rancher but she was making what clearly were some hard points, one of her hands moving from time to time in a chopping motion. Stedman, for his part, seemed almost to be placating her. After a time the man and woman moved away from the bank and its very faint lamplight.

At almost the same time a buggy drawn by two running horses came turning onto the top of the main street. Because there were so few lights other than those deliberately positioned, Cobb called out loudly and moved on to the street, waving his arms. The buggy came on.

Stedman, however, glimpsing one of its occupants, recognized her as his sister. Cobb now thought it was Emily Voller who was driving. Stedman now ran out, calling for the buggy to be stopped. A third of the way along the street, it was brought to a halt.

Cobb, already out of breath, came jogging to it. Beddoes appeared from somewhere. Stedman, not running but long-striding was already saying to his sister, 'Jane, yuh got to git off this street! From now on, anything can happen!'

Before the woman could utter a reply, Matt Jenner's harsh voice could be heard from atop the roof next to the mercantile.

'He's on that roof!'

Taber, in taking another cautious look over the parapet to find out what all the shouting was about, must have moved at the wrong time. And now, excited by what he saw as a chance, and although the man had ducked down, Jenner let fly a lashing rifle shot, sending heavy lead banging into the wooden parapet across the street. This brought an immediate response from Stedman down in the street.

'Goddamn it! Don't risk the hostage!' He had put Jenner up there for one purpose only. To get a clear shot only when he was sure that the target was Taber. Phena Radich was calling out, too, from somewhere, sounding as though she was close to breaking point. Someone must have gone to her, for she soon quietened down.

Matt Jenner then made his second mistake. He stood up. He looked down to try to see where Sam Stedman was and to observe the buggy that had arrived. Taber, the Remington gripped in his right fist, propped on top of the parapet, left hand grasping the right wrist for stability, shot at the man opposite. It was a long one, in bad light and Taber did not back himself to get a hit. But Jenner was whacked by the lead and dropped his rifle. It fell over the edge and first struck an awning, below, then clattered on to the street. Jenner himself went staggering away across the roof and fell down out of Taber's sight.

Stedman was now yelling for the buggy to be got off the street. Beddoes was calling on S-Bar men to watch closely for any move Taber might make. There was a strong sense, now, of matters coming to a head. Stedman's first purpose was to get both of the women out of harm's way and in particular to make sure that his sister not be exposed in any way to John Taber. That she was down off the buggy trying to get his attention, tugging at his sleeve, Stedman was choosing to ignore. But when they had retreated to the doorway of a feed and grain, he did say. 'I sent Augie Leech to hold yuh back on S-Bar.'

Emily, still very angry, broke in. 'Oh, we met Mr Leech. He wouldn't be persuaded to let us come here peaceably. When he made to draw his pistol I gave him a taste of the whip. Twice. I doubt that he's seeing so well. He's along the trail somewhere. If he manages to get into Charon, likely I'll give him another cut.'

Stedman was taken aback. Perhaps because Emily had spoken out so strongly, Jane Reed said, 'Sam, you've got to listen to me. You've got to hear this. I . . . I believe John Taber might have been wrongly accused.'

Beddoes, appearing at Stedman's elbow, heard it and was quick to say, 'Miz Reed, that jes' can't be. Taber, or Rolt, or whatever his damn' handle turns out to be, he got a fair trial. You was there at the time, Miz Reed. Yuh heard what was said, all through, ma'am. Yuh said different yourself, then.'

'I know that, Mr Beddoes, but — '

'Jane, yuh got to leave this man Taber to us.'

Beddoes nodded vigorously. 'An' we got to git these here ladies off'n the street.' And he added, 'Miz Voller, your man, he's been lookin' for yuh all over.'

'Mr Beddoes, that's strictly a matter between him and me. Where do you suggest we go now? Apart from the mercantile.'

It was the county sheriff's turn to be set back a pace, but he recovered fast. 'We'd best all go down to the county office. But we'll need to go 'way around this here block. It ain't no ways safe along Main.'

While not believing that either she or Jane Reed would be in any danger from John Taber, Emily said nothing, and followed Beddoes, Sam Stedman and Jane Reed.

Taber was aware that there had been some activity on the roof across the way but he did not consider shooting. He assumed that men had gone up there to help the rifleman down. Once, Taber thought he had heard the man call out in pain. Now, Dave Radich was gesturing at the gag and was starting to cough. Taber told him. 'I'll take it off. But open your yap just once and I'll lay a barrel on your other ear. It wouldn't be a wise move to try me out.' Radich, wide-eyed, nodded. Taber undid the bandanna. Its main purpose had been served anyway, keeping Radich's mouth shut during the time that Taber was getting him up on the roof.

Now Taber was much more interested in making the leap from this roof to the next one, taking the risk that men on the ground would hear them and realize what they were up to. Radich was to go first and when Taber told him that, he did not want any part of it.

'Goddamn it, Taber, a man could fall an' bust his neck!'

Taber wagged the Remington very close to Radich's face. 'Better than having your fool head laid open with this. Now back off, take a run at it, an' *go*. Soon as you're across, back off out of my way.' Taber realized that it was not the distance that was worrying Radich but the darkness up there.

The small group had arrived in the county office, entering a room where light seemed unnatural. It was in here that the argument between Sam Stedman and Jane Reed started up again. Emily Voller was tired and irritated and shaken from the encounter with Augie Leech, but she did not want to leave. She feared that if she should do so Jane Reed's resolve might crumble in the face of Sam Stedman's overbearing strength and Beddoes' thick-headed compliance with anything that Stedman promoted. So Emily stayed.

Jane Reed said, 'Sam, we've just got to talk about the stage robbery.'

'Yuh gave evidence yourself, Jane. It was Taber.'

'The passenger, the one who fired the pistol, gave most of the evidence. He thought he'd hit the man. I doubt that he did. But I spoke, going along with what he'd said. He *did* shoot. Mr Taber *was* found some way along that trail and he had a wound in his side. He claimed he'd been shot by a horseman, riding fast. That was probably the man who'd held us up.

And that man, whoever he was, had called out to the Wells Fargo messenger and to the driver of the stage. Mr Taber gave evidence in court. His voice bothers me. I can't believe it was the same voice as the one I'd heard at the hold-up. I wasn't at all sure, then; I'm even less sure now. And my possessions were never found. They certainly weren't with Mr Taber.'

'In somethin' like this, yuh got to *be* sure. But that ain't important, anyways. Taber was put in Mr Beddoes' jail for a damn' good reason. A man was shot dead; Taber busted out of here. That's why he's wanted now.'

Hearing this twisted tale, Emily could not hold back. 'As I understand it, Mr Taber shot the man Josiah Gaul in defence of his own life. Even the stray dogs in Charon know that. Gaul came — was brought here to kill him.' When Stedman started to say something, Emily simply went on talking over him. 'And he didn't *break out* of the jail. He walked out.

These men were either too stupid to lock him in or they let him out deliberately so that he could be shot down *escaping*.'

Beddoes, his big face colouring, started to say, 'Now, look here — '

Phena Radich came in. She looked much older than her years. Her face was sunken and drawn, her eyes staring out of hollows. Whatever Dave Radich's reputation, Phena was his mother and it was as a mother that she was here. The men stood looking somewhat uncomfortable. The women went at once to Phena.

Phena said, 'Mr Beddoes, there's a lot going on out there now. I want to hear you say that, whatever you plan to do about Taber, my son will come to no harm. The fool who fired that rifle could just as easy have hit Dave. Now, Dave's been a troublemaker, sure, but he don't deserve to get shot.'

Emily, though she was sympathetic towards Phena, especially seeing the state of her, thought that to hear Dave

194

Radich talked of in terms as bland as these was absurd. *Troublemaker* scarcely met the case. Dave was not only a loudmouth when in drink, which was often, but was a dangerous bully, quick to lay hands on a firearm. That so far he had not killed anybody was astonishing.

It was not Beddoes but Stedman who spoke up.

'Phena, like I've said already we'll watch out fer Dave. His safety comes first. Mr Beddoes, he's real set on that. He's give out instructions. If that hadn't been so, Taber, he'd never have got inside that store there in the first place. But Taber could start loosin' off.' He looked now at Jane Reed. 'Which is why yuh ought to go back to the S-Bar.'

'No, not 'til what I came here to say is listened to.'

Apparently tired of it now and wanting to reassert his authority, Beddoes said, 'It's the county law that has to git this done. With some backing from

Mr Stedman's men. It's long past time all the palaverin' was finished. Every minute that goes by gives Taber a chance to make some move. Now, that's when a serious shoot could start. Then we dunno who's gonna stop one.' He nodded to Cobb who went to a gun-case, unlocked it and took down a two-barrelled shotgun. Cobb then went to a desk and from one of its drawers fetched out a box of red and brass cartridges. The desk already had on it some red and white waxboard boxes of .44 ammunition and a loaded Walker Colt pistol.

There was a step at the street door. Robert Voller came in looking as self-assured as usual and equally as bad tempered.

'By God, Emily, I been lookin' all over for yuh!'

'Now you've found me.' There was no warmth in either voice. Those in the office exchanged glances.

'I want yuh to come with me. Come

home with me right now,' Voller said heavily. The fact that there were all these others here seemed not to have occurred to him.

'No.' Emily's reply was flat, emotionless.

'Emily, I got to insist — ' Voller, his face whitening with anger took a pace towards her. Emily stepped across to the cluttered desk and in both her narrow hands picked up the Walker Colt and awkwardly cocked it. Voller, looking at the black eye of it, stopped. 'Emily — !'

Beddoes, perturbed, half raising a hand, said, 'That thing ain't safe!'

'All the more reason for you to back off, Robert.' She was stony-faced, quite determined. 'I'll never be struck again by you or any other man. Take one more step and they'll carry you out. I mean it.' Ashen-faced now, humiliated, Voller turned away and left the office, stumbling out into the night. 'And you, Mr Beddoes,' Emily said, 'if you refuse to listen to what Mrs Reed's said, you'll only have to hear it later in another court of law. You won't come out of it well.'

But Beddoes did not want to be swayed; especially, Emily thought, by a woman. Even an armed woman.

'I got to git to Taber an' disarm the man. After what's happened, I cain't do nothin' else.'

'He's right, Mrs Voller,' Stedman said. 'Whatever might come out of it, after, he's right.'

Emily lowered the pistol. Beddoes reached across and with extraordinary gentleness, took it and put it back on the desk.

Dave Radich, having crossed successfully to the next roof, backed off. Taber launched himself across the alley-gap. He did not get it quite right, the toe of one boot catching the edge of the other roof. It was not much but enough to send him sprawling, though still gripping the pistol as he went rolling over and over. Dave Radich, aware that Taber still had hold of the pistol, did not approach him. But he smashed one of his boots through the glass of a skylight, and with the boot swept away jagged pieces. By the time a slightly dazed Taber realized what had happened, Radich had dropped through and was gone.

13

They were just outside the county office, the lawmen, Sam Stedman and the three women when there came a shout from 'way along the main street. Because of the line of lanterns set out on the street itself, and the paucity of lights elsewhere, it was virtually impossible to see anything that might be happening down there in the velvet dark. The shouting (the words indistinguishable) welled up, then suddenly ceased.

Beddoes said to the women, 'You'll be safer back in the building. Somethin's goin' on down there.'

Slowly they moved back in, but just beyond the doorway, all three stopped. There were chairs in the office but nobody wanted to sit. Uncertainty, tension, was heavy in the air.

Not much more than a minute after

that, a cowboy of the S-Bar came jogging out of the shadows, seeking his employer. What the rider had to tell them caused a stir.

'Dave Radich, he's got away!'

'Where's Taber?' This was Beddoes.

'Crossed over to the roof next door to that'n he was on. Fell down, he did. That's how Dave got away.'

'Where's Dave?'

'Way down there, t'other end o' Main, last I seen. Mad as a whole swarm o' hornets, Dave is. Took Matt Jenner's belt an' pistol.'

Clearly Stedman, for one, did not fancy the sound of that at all. And Harve Beddoes certainly didn't. With Dave Radich under Taber's pistol it had been less likely that the man they wanted would have been able to move very far or very quickly, even if he had managed to get out of the empty store. Now that Taber was on his own he could turn out to be a much bigger problem. But another matter for great concern was that the unpredictable Dave Radich had armed himself, and God alone knew where he had got to or what he might do. When the S-Bar rider then mentioned that in the course of arming himself, Dave had also taken the opportunity to help himself to a bottle from the nearest saloon, Beddoes wasn't slow to see the increased danger to all concerned.

'We got to locate Dave right soon. Cain't have that boy roamin' 'round out there on the prod. I gotta find out fast where Dave's at.' What he did not say was that he would prefer to have Dave Radich in the cage, cooling off. For Dave's whiskey-fuelled rage over his humiliation at the hands of John Taber would scarcely be controllable in any other way.

Hardly had this come into Beddoes' mind than they all heard the sound of a pistol going off somewhere in Charon. Certainly not anywhere near where they were. Careless of passing through lamplight, Beddoes, Cobb and Stedman began jogging along the middle of the street, followed by the S-Bar cowboy. The women had come again to the doorway of the county office, unable to stand inside, waiting, wondering what was happening. Phena Radich looked as though she might soon be physically sick.

There came now the sound of a horse arriving at the county office end of the main street, not coming quickly, loping along. It was brought to a halt at the tie-rail outside the county building. Someone who had been mounted up behind the man in the saddle now slid down over the horse's rump. The rider, too, dismounted and hitched the horse and came into the reach of the lamplight from the doorway. He made a head movement to the one who had dismounted first.

Deputy Nate Cooper looked tired but not displeased. The rider who had slid down from behind the cantle now came hesitantly forward. Probably Phena Radich recognized her, though Jane Reed and Emily Voller didn't. A dark-haired, black-eyed young woman, she was wearing a shabby brown dress with a ragged hem. Nell Rorke. The deputy took her by the arm and brought her inside the office, the other women giving them room.

Cooper said, 'This here's Nell Rorke from Mavor Creek.'

'I know who she is,' Phena said, clearly not pleased to see the young woman.

Nell asked, 'Where's Dave? What's happenin'?' No coquetry apparent now.

Phena said, 'Dave was took by John Taber. He's got away. We don't know where he is. But what he don't need right now is you here.'

'He sure don't, at that,' Cooper said. From a shirt pocket he took a small object and held it out for Jane Reed to look at. 'Yours?'

The woman blinked as though not believing what she was seeing. 'My brooch! My brooch that was taken at the hold-up! Mr Cooper, where did you get that?'

'From this woman,' Cooper said. 'Now, Nell, you tell 'em how yuh come by it.' The young woman did not want to. Cooper said, 'Nell?'

Finally, looking at the floor, she said, 'Dave, he give it to me.'

'When?' Cooper asked. 'Say when it was.'

Nell shifted and looked as though soon she might start to cry. 'After that stage got held up.'

Cooper then led her through the office and down the passage and locked her in a cell. 'Cain't afford to have her wanderin' around.' To Jane Reed he said, 'Got to keep that brooch 'til all this gits cleared up.'

'I understand.' Having taken it from him to look at, she now handed it back.

Emily, her face very pale, said, 'Mr Cooper, you have to look for Mr Beddoes right now. Dave Radich is out there, armed, and by now probably half drunk. He'll be looking for John Taber. And any one of a dozen men might take the chance to shoot Taber down.'

Even as she spoke, more pistol shots sounded. Nate Cooper went out, untied the horse and remounted.

Taber was in a corner. He had followed Dave Radich down off the roof and out into the darkness of a cluttered yard, but in his dazed condition, by the time he got there, Dave had vanished. Now, the Remington pistol in hand, Taber, having worked his way along a back street, became aware of men up ahead of him and suddenly, others who were some fifty yards behind. Taber did not wait around but ran to his left, stumbling inside a freight yard. He was tired and the shoulder he had hurt out in the brushlands when he had had to go diving off the horse had stiffened up and was paining him. Pistols stabbed the dark, tracking him. Heavy lead came hammering into a stout gatepost a mere foot away from him. Somewhere he could hear somebody yelling. Taber recognized the voice. Dave Radich.

'Taber, where the hell are yuh? Yuh bastard! Jailbird! Come git me now, mister! Now I got my hand filled! Missed yuh twice, but I ain't gonna miss yuh ag'in.' Taber assumed this meant the rifleman's attempt at him, out in the brushlands. And outside the rooming-house.

Almost on top of that, another voice could be heard, deeper and rougher than Radich's. Beddoes'.

'Cobb! Where the hell are yuh, Cobb? Tell Dave to hand that pistol over! An' S-Bar, back off!' Cooper had located Beddoes and spoken urgently to him. Consternation reigned.

Stedman's voice now called, 'S-Bar, do like the sheriff says! Back off! Git back on Main! Let Taber be!'

Cobb's voice, much closer to the freight yard where Taber was now crouching besides a heavy wagon, called, 'Dave . . . ?'

Another shot from a pistol split the night. A shotgun thumped and spat bluish flame. Cobb. Another pistol shot. A cry.

Then, 'What in the name o' God's goin' on?'

Stedman's voice yelled, 'Mr Cobb's been shot!'

Boots could be heard. Men running. Another pistol shot. From the dark of the freight yard, Taber called, 'Beddoes? This is Taber.'

There was a huddle of indistinct figures around another man lying on the street. A man detached himself from this group. This was Beddoes. He came a few paces towards the freight yard. Another man followed him.

Beddoes said, 'Yuh got my word Taber . . . there'll be no hand ag'in yuh now. Not here. Not in this county.'

Nate Cooper was the man who had followed Beddoes. 'John, I brung in Nell Rorke. Them fellers down on Mavor Creek thought twice about turnin' a badge away. Nell had a brooch that was stole from Miz Reed. Ain't no doubt, now, about who it was held up that stage. Dave was there at the soddies right after.'

A wave of relief swept through Taber. But there was anger there, too. But he said, 'Is that Cobb that's down?' There seemed to be no great urgency in seeking help for the deputy.

'Aaron Cobb's dead,' said Beddoes. 'Now we got to find Dave Radich.'

Taber came out and walked with Nate Cooper along the back street. Sam Stedman, for once absolutely quiet, walked with his men back towards Main. The body of Deputy Cobb was being carried, in a sagging u among them. When, with their burden, they got on to Main, Trubshawe was waving urgently to Beddoes.

'Seen Dave Radich runnin' like his ass was afire, But once he got by them lanterns up there I lost sight of 'im. What's goin' on? Where's Taber?'

'It's Radich I want,' Beddoes said. 'There's serious information been laid ag'in Dave. Taber's gone with Nate Cooper, lookin' fer the young bastard.

Dave, if he sees Taber, he'll be bound to make a try fer 'im.'

'Then may God Hisself help Dave.'

'Indeed.' Albert Stroud, the banker, wearing a pale derby hat and a chesterfield with a velvet collar, had come quietly to them. 'Mr Rolt, to be precise.' His thick-lensed eyeglasses were glinting.

'Yuh know about Rolt?' Beddoes asked.

'I've known about him for some while,' Stroud said. 'Even he does not know. But a prudent banker often makes discreet inquiries concerning account holders. In the strictest confidence, of course. I must say I believe it has been most unwise to push Mr Rolt to such lengths.'

'Well, I'll be damned,' Beddoes said. Then he moved away as fast as a man of his build could, heading up the main street. It had occurred to him — and also to Stedman at about the same time — that the women were still up at the county office and ought to

be told not to come out while Dave
Radich's whereabouts were unknown.
There could well be more shooting. The
death of Cobb had shaken Beddoes.
And it had shaken Stedman, too. To
nowhere in particular, his voice carrying
into the night, he had begun calling
to Radich, hoping that he would be
heard.

'Dave! Give it up, Dave! Come on
in!'

It seemed a useless thing to be doing
and did not sound in the least like the
usually bullying Stedman. But Beddoes
went jogging on, gasping now from the
effort. They had just reached the county
building, Beddoes only five yards ahead
of the rancher, when Cooper and Taber
came walking on to Main from a side
street. They were not far from the still-
burning lanterns, long pistols glinting
in the eerie light. Trubshawe had come
along the opposite boardwalk to observe
events and as soon as he recognized
Taber he called out who he was. Taber
nodded, then he and Cooper, looking

all around, came slowly to the middle of the street. There was a sense of not knowing where to go next. The man they were looking for could be anywhere.

About fifty feet behind them, Dave Radich came to the edge of shadows. Trubshawe who was looking in that direction at the time, bawled a warning and flung his old bones full length on the boardwalk.

Taber and Nate Cooper turned at the same time, shooting, pistols flicking flame as Radich shot too, but he was already on the move, slipping to one side, back into shadows. Taber shot again but missed. Stedman was yelling for Radich to give up.

'It's no use no more!'

Radich shot again and lead raked Stedman, who had drawn no pistol, and the rancher cursed and slipped to one knee. Again Radich shot. Cooper was on his knees. He had been shot. Taber came walking across in front of him. Stedman was still shouting.

'Fer God's sake, Dave, put up the pistol!'

And incredibly, Phena Radich was outside too, screaming at her son. 'Dave! Dave!'

In turn, Beddoes was yelling for the woman to go back inside. Radich took no notice of any of them. He shot again at Taber. The lead flicked Taber's sleeve. Taber shot. The stink of gunsmoke was everywhere. Taber shot again. This time Radich went staggering away, then fell down. Taber was now walking in on him.

Phena, who was still there, was screaming, 'Don't kill my boy!'

Radich, still mostly in shadow, was on his hands and knees, head hanging. Taber saw the glint of the fallen pistol. Savagely he kicked it away.

Lanterns were now picked up and brought closer, Trubshawe carrying one, another held by the banker, Stroud. He went across to where Cooper lay. Cooper was alive. So was Radich, hit solidly in the left thigh and in considerable pain.

Taber seemed to lose interest. Moving away, he heard Stroud say quietly, 'Mr Rolt?'

'Rolt's dead,' Taber said. He squatted alongside Cooper. 'I'm real sorry it's come to this, Nate.'

One of the S-Bar riders came. With his help, Taber carried Cooper to a drugstore where lamps had now been turned up. Coming out, Taber saw that Emily Voller was there.

She said, 'You're all right?'

'Yes.'

'Phena told me you could have killed Dave, and didn't.'

He shrugged. 'If she says so.' Then, 'I'm still none the wiser about who set those boys on me, the first night. If it was Cobb, I'll never know it now. Or who it was paid Joshua Gaul. I guess that doesn't matter. Whoever it was has to live with it.'

Emily said, 'Phena went completely to pieces when the shooting began. You're not going to believe what came

214

out. Dave is Sam Stedman's son. That's why Stedman's been caring of Phena herself. But Dave himself doesn't know it. Now maybe Sam will do something openly about that. It was probably kept hidden because of his other ambitions. But no wonder he didn't want to see Dave killed. But John, he must have known it was Dave, at that stage. Even if he only found out later. I don't think Jane would ever have spoken up without being pushed to it. For different reasons, she and Sam must have been very afraid of what you might find out, coming back home.'

'Me an' Sam, we're gonna have to have a long talk. By now he must've guessed that it's to come. To begin with, I'll want that conviction taken out. Sam's about to be busy, talking with those in high places. Maybe he can start with the congressmen.'

She asked, 'Do you think Beddoes knew it all?'

'I doubt it. Beddoes reckons he's on safe ground as long as he's tight with

Stedman. Stedman didn't want to be seen as anything but clean an' upright. The leading light in the county. No past to worry him.' Then, 'Come on. I'll walk you to the corner.'

At once, she said, 'I'm not going that way. I'm not going home. I'm going to the Criterion Hotel. It's . . . oh, it's a long and none too pleasant story, John.'

'Then I'll walk you to the Criterion.'

She slid a hand inside his arm and they walked away. More lamps were coming on in Charon.

THE END

THE CROOKED SHERIFF
John Dyson

Black Pete Bowen quit Texas with a burning hatred of men who try to take the law into their own hands. But he discovers that things aren't much different in the silver mountains of Arizona.

THEY'LL HANG BILLY
FOR SURE:
Larry & Stretch
Marshall Grover

Billy Reese, the West's most notorious desperado, was to stand trial. From all compass points came the curious and the greedy, the riff-raff of the frontier. Suddenly, a crazed killer was on the loose — but the Texas Trouble-Shooters were there, girding their loins for action.

RIDERS OF RIFLE RANGE
Wade Hamilton

Veterinarian Jeff Jones did not like open warfare — but it was there on Scrub Pine grass. When he diagnosed a sick bull on the Endicott ranch as having the contagious blackleg disease, he got involved in the warfare — whether he liked it or not!

BEAR PAW
Nevada Carter

Austin Dailey traded two cows to a pair of Indians for a bay horse, which subsequently disappeared. Tracks led to a secret hideout of fugitive Indians — and cattle thieves. Indians and stockmen co-operated against the rustlers. But it was Pale Woman who acted as interpreter between her people and the rangemen.